"I wouldn't have bothered you if I didn't think it was important."

"What else could possibly—"

"Erin, I think you're in danger," Jason said.

"Okay, Jason. Whatever game you're playing, I'm leaving. It's been a long night. Please go."

"You know me well enough to know this isn't a game."

The truth was she didn't know this Jason at all. People changed.

"Another wife of a guy on my team died early this morning."

"This has nothing to do with me."

"There's more. My buddy Cole Dawson's ex-wife was also found dead. Three spouses in one day? From the same team? A team whose last mission might cause someone to want revenge? Until somebody figures out how they got their intel, I can't promise whoever this is doesn't know about you, too."

Jodie Bailey writes novels about freedom and the heroes who fight for it. Her novel *Crossfire* won a 2015 RT Reviewers' Choice Best Book Award. She is convinced a camping trip to the beach with her family, a good cup of coffee and a great book can cure all ills. Jodie lives in North Carolina with her husband, her daughter and two dogs.

FATAL RESPONSE

JODIE BAILEY

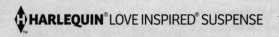

HARLEQUIN® LOVE INSPIRED® SUSPENSE

 LOVE INSPIRED BOOKS

Recycling programs for this product may not exist in your area.

ISBN-13: 978-1-335-54401-8

Fatal Response

Copyright © 2018 by Jodie Bailey

www.Harlequin.com

Printed in U.S.A.

Thou hast covered me in my mother's womb. I will praise thee; for I am fearfully and wonderfully made: marvellous are thy works; and that my soul knoweth right well.
—*Psalms* 139: 13b-14

To all of my MilSpouse Friends...
For the times you've made a home where you never wanted to go, celebrated holidays with your loved ones far away, rearranged your life for the "needs of Uncle Sam" and planned reunions that never seemed to go quite right but turned out perfectly anyway... You are more amazing than the world will ever understand. I'm honored to stand beside you.

ONE

The chrome of Fire Engine 7 gleamed in the glow of the dim lights hanging overhead. Erin Taylor ran one finger along the grille of the monstrous vehicle, then buffed the streak off with her sleeve. She could bust out a rag and work on it, but she'd done that an hour ago. Since she was the only person pulling overnight duty in the station of the Mountain Springs Volunteer Fire Department, there wasn't anyone but herself to come along and undo her work.

Great. The dark hours were stretching longer than usual, and it wasn't even midnight. Maybe it had to do with knowing where she could be right now…at a weekend training conference in Nashville. But she'd had to pass the opportunity along to Mark Jennings so her father wouldn't be left alone for an entire weekend. His safety came first, even if it sometimes hindered her career...or derailed her life.

Not that things were ever going to change. Dwelling on it would only make her feel worse.

Drumming her fingers on her thighs, she wandered to the large garage doors at the front of the building and stared through the windows into the darkness. Mountain Springs slept quietly about a mile away. They hadn't had a call in a couple of nights, not even for a medical emergency. On this moonless autumn evening, everything was still.

But a growing restlessness had her prowling the station. She'd organized the small kitchen. Considered baking brownies. Had tried to sleep on the small bed in the bunk room at the end of the hall. Every time she settled in and closed her eyes, something drove her to her feet.

The same kind of instinct had kicked in when the woods north of town caught fire in a lightning storm a couple of years ago. Her subconscious had caught the scent of smoke before her nose realized it was there. She'd already been halfway to the station when the alarm sounded.

There was no smoke tonight, simply a weird twinge in her gut that kept her from relaxing.

It probably had to do with *the car*.

For nearly two weeks, an older dark sedan had turned into the front parking lot of the station, turned around and left. The engine never shut off. The driver never left the vehicle. Each time, the only indication the car was there was headlights sweeping through the windows on the bay doors as the car made its turn.

She'd mentioned the car to her cousin Wyatt, a Mountain Springs police officer, at lunch after church on Sunday. They'd ultimately decided it was a new parent with a sleep-resistant infant.

Still, the random drive-bys poked at her creepy-meter a little bit.

With a slight shudder, Erin checked the front door for the third time to make sure it was locked. The back door was as tight as the front, the music of crickets and frogs drifting in from the back of the building.

Erin pivoted on her heel to go back to the office. There were always grant proposals to write. As one of two paid members of the mostly all-volunteer department, the bulk of the office work fell to her. At least it made the nights go faster.

A muffled scrape crept through the back door. Erin leaned toward the sound. She'd strapped bungee cords on the large trash cans to keep the critters out. With the fire station situated on the edge of a broad mountain meadow, all kinds of wild animals drifted past the building. She'd seen everything from adorable baby raccoons to black bears that could swat her into eternity with one swipe of a massive paw.

One time of having to clean trash strewn across the property by an unseen animal when she was a rookie volunteer had been enough to make her double-check the security of those trash cans.

Still, the heavy plastic likely wouldn't be able to withstand a bear. If the noise continued, she could always flip on the lights and scare the creature across the meadow and into the woods.

Hand on the switch, she listened, the hairs on the back of her neck standing at attention.

Tires screeched on the road to the station, and headlights swept across the doors of the bay. An engine revved as it strained through the gears.

Somebody was flying along the short road that ended at the station. There'd been problems in the past with drag racers on the straightest stretch of road in the county, but the presence of the fire station had put a stop to racing when it was built twelve years earlier. With at least one firefighter constantly on duty, even the craziest of kids was smart enough to know a quick race would end in a phone call to the police.

Whoever was out there was coming in hot.

Lord, help me if they're bringing in an injured child. With the closest hospital nearly half an hour away, it wouldn't be the first time a Mountain Springs resident had forgone 911 to bring their emergency straight to the nearest help.

Flipping on the outside floodlights, Erin shoved open the back door as a small red sports car slid to a halt in the center of the rear parking lot. The driver's door flew open, and a young woman jumped out. She spotted Erin and hefted a large padded envelope over her head. "Don't hurt him! Please!"

Someone must be in the back seat of the car. Erin stepped away from the building. "Is someone in the car who needs—"

"I came alone." Her voice shook, pleading as she held the envelope out toward Erin, although a good twenty feet separated them. "Please. Just…please."

Erin eased back toward the building and snaked her hand behind her, feeling for the door handle. If this stranger was high or on a mental break she needed assistance, but she could easily turn violent. "Ma'am? Can I help you with—"

"Don't hurt him!" The woman rounded her car and stepped cautiously toward Erin, holding out the package. "Please, I don't know—"

An engine roared and tires screamed as another car accelerated and skidded around the side of the building.

It was the dark sedan that had driven by so many times.

The stranger's eyes widened in panic. She froze, directly in the path of the oncoming headlights.

Adrenaline streaked in a flashover through Erin as she took two steps away from the building.

The car's engine revved higher as it swerved toward the woman.

It wasn't slowing. Throwing her hands over her head, Erin tried to yell a warning, but her throat constricted. *No! Stop!* There was no way this was happening. Nothing she could do to prevent it.

Time slowed. A dull, crunching thud tore the air as the dark four-door slammed into the young woman. Her body was hurled limply onto the hood of the car. The windshield cracked into a spiderweb from the impact of her head. She dropped to the ground and rolled.

The sedan skidded around the corner of the building and disappeared in a shriek of tires, leaving behind the sharp smell of tire rubber and an unearthly silence.

Erin's breath came in hard gasps. A ringing in her ears drowned out the silence as the horror of the past minute gripped her in a momentary paralysis. Her mind screamed she should run, curl into a ball, call for help…

But she was the help.

Her training took over. Alert for sounds of the other vehicle's return, Erin bolted for the broken body crumpled on the ground. *Lord, let there be a pulse. Breathing. Anything.*

She dropped to her knees and let her gaze sweep the victim who lay on her side, eyes staring vacantly into the darkness.

Swallowing a cocktail of grief and fear, Erin reached out to search for a pulse she was certain she would never find.

Footsteps pounded on the pavement at the far side of the building. The sound rocked Erin back on her heels and she whipped toward the approaching steps, her mind racing with prayers and fear.

A figure appeared at the dark corner, running toward her. In the shadows, she couldn't make out features, could only tell it was a man. But there was something familiar—

And then the man was awash in light, the silence shattered by the sound of an engine roaring closer.

There was no time to think.

Army Sergeant First Class Jason Barnes sprinted toward the woman who stood silhouetted in the headlights of the oncoming car, refusing to question if he could outrun the vehicle sliding around the corner of the fire station with its engine revving into a high whine as it accelerated.

He couldn't allow anyone else to die on his watch.

The roar of the engine grew closer, the lights brighter. He'd never make it. He'd never reach her in time. The car was too fast.

The ache in his knee made him too slow.

He was a couple of meters from her when tires screeched and rubber burned. The vehicle skidded sideways to a halt, scraping the passenger door against the brick building.

At the same moment, Jason reached the woman and grabbed her by the waist, dragging her with him to safety behind the Mustang belonging to his buddy Seth's wife, which sat at an odd angle on the concrete.

They were safe…unless the driver got out and came after them.

He looked over his shoulder, shielding the woman, as the rear tires spun and the dark older-model sedan skidded around the side of the building, the driver nothing more than a hulking shadow in a fleeting glimpse through the rear window.

Then the woman he'd rescued, the one he still held to his chest with one arm, repaid him for saving her life by driving her head into the side of his jaw. "Let me go."

Shock relaxed his hold and she stumbled forward, barely catching herself by planting both hands on the trunk of Angie's car. She regained her balance, then turned toward him with all of the suddenness of a summer tornado.

A very familiar tornado.

The air left his lungs in a rush, and he had to dig deep for enough air to say her name. "Erin?"

For the first time, her eyes met his, her face shadowed by the floodlights behind her. But there was no doubt, none at all

He'd rescued his ex-wife.

For a moment, there was zero sign of recognition, but then her eyes widened and she gasped. "What are…? Where did you come from?" She backed away from him slowly, glancing over her shoulder, then back to him as her jaw set in something that might be fear. "Did you do this?"

"Do what? Save your life?" Wait. No. This was not about them. He couldn't let this become the discussion he'd played out in his head for years.

He had to find Angie Daniels, and Erin had been standing in front of Angie's Mustang while a second car bore down on her.

Angie's car, Erin beside it. Nothing computed. Right now, he couldn't focus on the parts that didn't make sense. He had to focus on finding Seth's wife.

Staff Sergeant Seth Daniels had called the members of their team an hour earlier and asked them to search the county for Angie because it was too soon for the police to get involved. All the man knew was he'd awakened from a dead sleep a few minutes after midnight to find his wife and her car missing.

Jason had stopped at Seth's and taken his buddy's phone in order to track Angie's whereabouts with an app her husband had installed. When the team had returned from Iraq a few months earlier, bruised and wounded, the paranoia had hit them all. Dogged by rumors of retaliation by some of the terror cells they'd infiltrated, each man had done what it took to make sure his family was safe.

Those safety measures included knowing where their loved ones were at all times.

The trail had stopped here, at the Mountain Springs Volunteer Fire Department. And now Jason stood by Angie's car...with a woman he'd never imagined he'd see again. A woman who was accusing him of... Of what? "Where's the person who was driving this car?"

Erin didn't answer, simply turned her back to jog to the front of Angie's vehicle, where she knelt so he could no longer see her.

"I asked you a question, Erin. I need an answer. How did this car get here?" He rounded the rear of the Mustang and stalked toward Erin, who bent over something on the ground. "Where's the woman who...?" His gaze fell on a familiar pair of boots splayed on the pavement. On a growing dark pool at Erin's feet.

No.

It couldn't be.

This was a nightmare. The helplessness of his history leaking its way into his subconscious. There was no other way any of this made sense, the only way so many incongruous pieces of his life could be packed together on the cement drive of a back-road fire station. The only way Erin could be in front of him, her head bent over Angie's body.

"Tell me she's alive." Because if she wasn't, he couldn't do it. He couldn't call Seth and tell him his wife, the woman whose existence had kept Seth alive in the dark days after the incident overseas had nearly killed them all, was gone.

Erin rose and turned to walk toward him, her boots leaving dark imprints on the shadowed ground.

Jason didn't want to think about what those tracks were made of. He tried to step around Erin, but she blocked his view and pressed a hand to his chest, backing him around the rear of the car. "Don't look. If you know her at all… Don't look." She'd slipped into the cold professional mask he'd seen on her one too many times, the one that said she'd seen horrors he couldn't unsee for her.

The one that said she was protecting a victim's family.

The one that told him Angie Daniels was dead.

TWO

Erin pressed her palms to the wall and stared out the narrow window in the fire exit in the station's kitchen. Huge portable lights shone over the parking lot and onto the edges of the grassy meadow the department used for training behind the fire station. The Mustang still sat on the asphalt, a white sheet covering the remains of the woman Jason had referred to as Angie.

Having a name made everything so much harder. Angie. Who knew Jason. Who had been ripped from the world in a brutal, horrifying way. Whose death Erin would never be able to unsee.

Erin had responded to accident scenes and sick calls, had been trained to render aid in the most dire circumstances, but she had never been present when life was violently torn away. It was a whole different scenario.

Her stomach churning, Erin leaned her

forehead against the shatterproof glass and looked for something else to focus on. At the far corner of the parking lot, Jason was talking to a police officer who had his back to her. From this distance, it was tough to tell who the officer was.

Erin turned her back on the high window in the dayroom and walked to the center of the kitchen. She was tired. Exhausted in a way she hadn't been in years. All she wanted was to cross the hall to the bunk room and collapse, but she couldn't. She'd given her statement, which had served to solidify the horror in her mind, and if she closed her eyes there was no doubt the sickening sights and sounds of Angie Daniels's final moments would overtake her.

So would the memory of intense blue eyes that still somehow managed to see straight through her.

There was a time when her heart would have known Jason Barnes was living half an hour away.

Even better, there was a time when he'd have been sitting with her on the small couch on the other side of the room, cramming his mouth with popcorn while they binge-watched cheesy eighties television.

Everything could have been different if

he'd understood her side of the story. But he never had and, in the end, he'd simply thrown up his hands and walked away.

Hands shaking, Erin grabbed the pot from the coffee maker and turned on the water in the sink to fill it, but she misjudged the distance and clanked the metal carafe against the faucet, dropping it with a clatter.

There wasn't enough reserve left to care. Instead, she lowered her chin to her chest and stared at the gray tile floor.

Her eyes slipped shut against the mist threatening to build into full-on tears. She was not crying. Not now. Never where anyone might see.

"I see you're handling tonight's events well."

Erin jumped at the deep masculine voice behind her, then relaxed when she found the source. "Tonight's not the night to sneak up on me, Wyatt."

Her cousin bent and grabbed the pot, then set it in the sink. The badge on his black Mountain Springs Police Department jacket gleamed in the fluorescent lights overhead. "Wasn't trying to. You just looked like you could use some—"

"I don't need help." Snatching the carafe, she shoved it under the water and waited for it to fill. "I need coffee. You want coffee?"

Truth was, with her hands shaking and mind racing, coffee was the last thing she needed, but it would give her something to do until he left. Wyatt Stephens had a way of figuring out all of her hidden secrets. It was one of the reasons her cousin was the only person who knew she'd once been married to Jason. If she'd tried to keep him in the dark, he'd have figured it out. He read her almost as well as Jason did.

The difference was, Wyatt's ability to read her mind came from growing up together. Jason's came from a whole other kind of relationship.

Erin balled her fists to keep from digging her fingers into her scalp. She didn't need Jason Barnes in her headspace.

"I just got here, but I wanted to check on you before I headed to the crime scene." Wyatt laid a hand on her shoulder to keep her from turning her back fully to him. "You want to talk about it? What you saw—"

"Was something I couldn't stop." Her stomach knotted as the horrible crunching thud seemed to echo in the room. She didn't want to talk about the collision either. A woman was dead because Erin hadn't been able to rescue her. It was her job. She'd failed.

"That's twice you've cut me off in the past

thirty seconds." With a gentle tug, Wyatt turned her to face him. He took the carafe from her hand and set it behind her on the counter. "What else is happening? You don't usually—"

"I don't usually see helpless women get purposely mowed down."

"That's three times."

With a sigh, Erin pulled away from her cousin's grip and leaned back against the counter, shoving her hands into her pockets as she stared at the black leather couch across the room. "Jason's here."

It took a second for the name to register, but she could tell when it sank in. Wyatt's chin lifted slightly. "Why?"

"I have no idea." Erin ran over the brief encounter, leaving out the part where the sight of him had driven her back half a decade.

"Did he say how long he's staying?"

She shook her head as her phone vibrated in the thigh pocket of her navy blue uniform pants. After pulling it out, she read the screen.

Heard there was some excitement. You headed home early? We're out of coffee.

Why was her father awake at 1:12 a.m.? And why couldn't he, just once, ask about her? She was half tempted to shoot back an I'm fine, Dad, thanks for asking.

Instead, Erin shoved her phone into her pocket while Wyatt watched with a raised eyebrow.

"You could head home, you know."

"Chief Kelliher is on his way back from out of town, so I'm in charge even if the station is offline during the investigation. I'd rather stay here anyway. At least then there'd be a chance at sleep instead of..." Instead of cleaning whatever mess her father had decided to leave for her, running through the inevitable argument about why she didn't find a regular day job, then mowing the huge two-acre lawn before she could drop into her own bed.

"Move out, Erin. Make him stand on his own two feet and stop treating you like his personal servant."

It was the same thing he'd been preaching since she'd turned eighteen. Jason had echoed him every time. The difference was, Jason had a greater stake in her moving out than Wyatt ever had.

Neither of them understood she couldn't simply walk away, so she'd stopped arguing. It was her fault her father suffered from the medical issues that held him back in life.

Her father had never liked Jason, had

deemed him trouble from the start. Maybe Erin should have listened instead of suggesting they elope the day after high school graduation…and drive to South Carolina in style in her father's prized '68 Camaro.

On the way home, a drunk driver ran them off the road at the bridge over Wisdom Creek. They'd tumbled down the embankment and come to rest in the creek, leaving the car destroyed, Jason with a concussion, and Erin with a broken leg and busted ribs.

Her father blamed Jason, and his anger skyrocketed, blowing in an explosion when Jason came to the house the day she got home from the hospital. Before either of them could confess their elopement, Erin's father had collapsed, the combination of his diabetes and his anger making him the victim of a stroke that had forced him into months of rehab and Erin into silence about her marriage.

It was her responsibility to take care of her father, but the one man who should have understood and supported her the most had never been able to understand. Jason had pushed her to tell the truth about their marriage so they could stop sneaking stolen moments together. He wanted to tell her father, to have her leave home and move in with him.

No, Jason had never understood. Her father had needed to be stronger first. Another blowup could have killed him.

She had to make it up to her father for wrecking his car and his life.

And he never let her forget it.

The radio on Wyatt's shoulder crackled. He tipped his head to listen, then glanced toward the door. "I have to go, but if you need me, I'm—"

"Only a phone call away?"

"That's four." Wyatt turned and walked out, his footsteps echoing through the outer office and into the hallway.

Erin stood in the tiny kitchen, lips pursed. There was too much energy in her twitching muscles. She needed to put them to work.

She strode through the office and across the hall into the bay. The low murmur of voices filtered in through the garage doors at the back of the building, but the distance was mercifully too far to pick out words.

The engine still gleamed from her earlier restlessness, so she grabbed her supplies and walked to the end of the row where the brush truck stood. Her lone footsteps echoed off the high ceiling, the familiarity as comforting as her own heartbeat. No matter what happened in her life, a firefighter was what she was meant to be. She knew it in silences like this as well as she knew it in turnout gear facing a fully engulfed structure.

A small smile edged up her face for the first time in hours, and she let her fingers trail along the side of the large red utility vehicle. She inspected hoses and dials, then dug into the bucket for an old toothbrush. Might as well hit those spots where nobody ever remembered to clean.

She was standing on the running board polishing a handrail when a door opened on the other side of the building. Footsteps, slow but steady, paced toward her.

It was probably Wyatt. He had never been able to understand *I don't want to talk*.

Lowering her hand, Erin grabbed the rail and turned, but she kept her place as she checked her watch. Over an hour on the truck. No wonder her neck ached as much as her heart.

The man who rounded the front of the ladder truck wasn't her cousin.

Jason.

Her fingers tightened on the handrail while she fought to keep her expression impassive, but her insides jolted at his unexpected appearance. In the fullness of the overhead lights, he was everything she remembered and a whole lot more. Those blue eyes had first caught her attention over a decade earlier. While they held concern, they lacked the warmth she'd once enjoyed. Instead, they were wiser and darker, as though they'd absorbed everything he'd seen on his many deployments. His thick sandy-blond hair was longer on the top, tousled, but the smooth skin at his neck said it had been recently cut.

He'd filled out over the past few years, his shoulders broader, his chest firmer beneath his creamy beige sweater. And while it was impossible, he even seemed to be a couple of inches taller.

His height made her glad she'd stayed on her perch on the brush truck. He'd always towered over her by several inches.

Warmth breezed through her with the memory. She'd loved the way her head tucked beneath his chin when he held her. It made her feel protected, like nothing could touch her. The outside world and all its troubles had always drifted far away.

"You okay?"

She blinked twice, warmth morphing to embarrassment. She was staring at him. Had been for who knew how long. Balling her free hand, Erin dug her nails into her palm and turned back to the truck, inspecting an invisible spot on a coupling. "I'm fine."

"And that's why you're polishing chrome in the dead of night?"

Jason's voice held a knowing it shouldn't. How often had he found her at the station doing the same thing? He'd always known where she'd run after an argument. He'd always found her.

Yeah. There would be no making up tonight or ever again. At least not with Jason Barnes.

She had to remind herself why it hadn't worked between them. He'd repeatedly tried to force her hand with her father, refusing to understand why she couldn't tell her dad the truth about their marriage. Jason had fought against her, not with her, and certainly not for her.

Armed with her catalog of reasons he was every bad idea in the world, she faced him. "What are you doing back in town?"

"Stationed at Camp McGee as an instructor. Got here about a month ago."

"A month. Were you going to warn me?" The words bit as the emotions of the night congealed into an overarching anger she couldn't harness. Jumping from the truck, she prepared to pour out every tirade she'd ever practiced in her mind.

But footsteps on the other side of the bay stopped her.

Jason turned toward the sound at the same time she did.

Wyatt rounded the corner with police chief Arch Thompson at his side, their expressions grim.

Erin tensed. Whatever was coming, it was clear…

Her world was about to tilt again.

"Meth?" Erin eyed the evidence bag police chief Arch Thompson held at his side.

The whole night was spinning faster, circling with all of the ferocity of a whirlpool that threatened to drag her under. Now it had bled into the small dayroom of the fire station. Her home away from home had been invaded by the carnage outside, with Chief Thompson adding more pieces to a story spinning so far out of control it was ceasing to make sense.

Tall and slim, Thompson looked more like a pro basketball player than a small-town police chief. But tonight, his typically smiling eyes were dark and troubled. He stood between the kitchenette and the couch in the dayroom, Wyatt beside him, the two men dominating the space. "Afraid so. And even more, there's—"

"No." Jason had been standing by the back door, silently watching the men. The rigid set of his shoulders and the corded muscles in his neck held a tension Erin hadn't seen since their last face-to-face conversation, right before he walked out the door forever. "No. Angie wasn't a courier. I'd have known. *We'd* have known."

Who was *we*? For the hundredth time in two hours, Erin wondered who Angie was to Jason. He seemed to walk a tightrope in his grief, one that fell to anger on one side and sorrow on the other. Underneath it all, though, there was an underlying something she couldn't quite get a read on. The full story was bigger than he was letting on.

"Erin says the suspect vehicle came by the station a few times, but has never hung around. She also says she saw Angie Daniels exit her vehicle tonight and hold up this envelope. Without testing I can't be a hundred percent positive, but having had more than our fair share of busts lately, I'm almost certain. This is crystal meth." Chief Thompson lifted the bag higher. "Convince me she was innocent."

Jason scrubbed his hand over his hair,

his expression drawn. "Angie was a straight arrow. A volunteer who kept spouses in the loop when the soldiers were deployed. One of those people who never had a bad mood. Nothing she ever did or said points to this."

"Why would she get out of the car telling me not to 'hurt him'?" The words were out before Erin could stop them. She had to say something, to defend the woman she'd failed to save. If she continued to keep silent, she'd find herself across the room with her arms around her ex-husband, trying to comfort him in the loss of whoever this woman was to him. It didn't settle well with her heart or with her stomach, if she was being perfectly honest. But no matter what had happened in the past or who they were now, she couldn't let Jason stand by and listen to more accusations against someone he obviously cared about. "And she was scared. Of me. There's no doubt in my mind."

"She could have been high." Wyatt's voice was low, almost as though he didn't want to say the words. When Jason straightened as though he was going to argue, Wyatt held up his hand to stop him. "I have to ask the hard question here, Jason, the one we're all thinking. Angie Daniels was married to your teammate, but you're awfully invested in this." He swallowed hard, glanced at Erin, then back at Jason. "Were the two of you—"

"No." The emphatic tone in Jason's voice left no room for argument.

Relief made Erin grab for the back of the couch, but recrimination soon followed. A woman was dead. Was she really concerned about how much Jason cared? Now? *Lord, give me back my right mind.* She sure wasn't getting through this night without His help.

Sinking to the edge of a recliner a few feet away from Erin, Jason rested his elbows on his knees and let his hands hang. He stared at the wall for a long time, almost as though he was watching a movie no one else in the room could see.

Chief Thompson shifted but said nothing as Wyatt leveled a hard gaze on Jason, the unspoken request for an explanation hanging heavy in the air. The two men had been best friends in high school, practically family after Jason's parents abandoned him and he filed for emancipation rather than go into the foster system. That had to be the reason Wyatt was here now, because Jason was hurting and he couldn't stand not to be there for the man who had been closer than a brother.

Although as far as Erin knew, the two hadn't spoken since Jason joined the army eight years earlier. When Jason left town for the army, he'd cut ties with everyone and left a lot of pain behind. The only one who knew how deeply personal it had been for Erin was Wyatt, and they'd done their best to carry each other through.

"We're a tight team. Tighter than most after…" Jason's voice seemed to come from far away, as though what he was saying came from deep inside, from a hidden place he didn't access often. "Six months ago, we had an incident where our commander was killed. Master Sergeant Jonathan Fitzgerald. Most of us were wounded, some worse than others." When he lifted his head, it was to look straight at Erin. "There's the short version of how a bunch of us were sent to Camp McGee. The army believes our experiences can help train other teams."

Not to mention give them time stateside to heal. The pain of what Jason wasn't saying seared Erin. There was definitely more to his story, and it bled out slowly in what he couldn't talk about. "It's made you a tighter family."

Though the words were soft, Jason caught them. He nodded a silent *thank you*, then stood and turned back to the two police officers. "There's nothing else to tell unless you know something else you need to tell me."

The quick look the chief and Wyatt exchanged made Erin brace herself against the back of the couch. The drugs were half of the issue.

"What?" Jason had seen it too.

"Mrs. Daniels's cell phone was unlocked, and there were messages indicating she'd been running drugs for a while. But her last message was the one we're concerned with now. It directed her to deliver the package to the firefighter on duty at the station by midnight, or someone would kill her husband."

THREE

"What?" Erin wavered, her fingers digging into the black leather sofa she'd been leaning against.

Instinctively, Jason reached for her, but he drew back as Wyatt stepped around him and laid a hand on Erin's shoulder.

Jason stood down. Right. He got it. Erin wasn't his to take care of anymore.

For the first time, he took a second to really look at her. She was the same yet so different. Her dark hair was longer and pulled back in a ponytail. She was more toned, although the uniform could be creating an illusion of strength. Still, she appeared way too delicate to be the rescue hero he knew her to be.

And the drive to protect her was strong, no matter what their past might say.

"Why?" The word was soft, as though it leaked from a deflating balloon. Erin brushed Wyatt's hand from her shoulder and stood taller, seeming to re-center herself. "I don't understand."

"Neither do we," Wyatt said. "Did you know her? Ever seen her before tonight?"

Erin shook her head slowly as though she were cataloging recent days as she answered. "No. Never. The sole connection is the car. I know it's the same one that's circled the parking lot a few times. There can't be two identical cars like that one in a town this small."

"Someone wanted you involved." Jason had no doubt. There was no way all of this was a coincidence. He'd built his career on analyzing the details, and these added up a little too well. Somehow, Erin was a target too.

The *why* made no sense, though. No more than Angie running drugs did. It was a setup. It had to be.

"Normally, I'd say you're reaching, but..." Arch Thompson was skeptical, and Jason couldn't blame him. Arch had been a senior when Jason, Erin and Wyatt were freshmen, but in a small town, everyone was acquainted with everyone. The young police chief had always been a good guy, if a little bit cocky, but in Jason's line of work, cocky could work for you.

"Jason." Wyatt cut into the conversation and held up his cell phone. "There are some men outside asking for you. Apparently, Staff Sergeant Daniels is here. You're free to go out and see them as long as you don't feed them any details past this was a hit-and-run."

Jason dug his fingers into his thighs. As much as he wanted to stay and make sure Erin was truly okay, the men outside needed him more. He had no doubt Seth had come to the station trying to get to his wife and no doubt the others had followed him. "Got it." He hesitated as he passed Wyatt and Erin. "Call me if you need anything else." Even he wasn't sure which of the two he was talking to.

Wyatt nodded. Erin didn't respond.

Not that he'd expected her to. The way the conversation had gone earlier, there was still a large gulf between them. One he had no idea how to bridge.

When he shoved through the door, the temperature was noticeably colder than it had been an hour or so earlier. He shoved his hands into the pockets of his jeans and strode toward the barriers at the road, where a handful of cars sat parked along the side of the road.

Only one person was in sight.

Jason ducked under the barrier and came up next to Staff Sergeant Alex "Rich" Richardson, who was leaning against the side of his pickup truck. Rich hardly acknowledged him as he scanned the wood line on the other side of the station. The vigilance never went away, even on home soil and especially tonight.

It might never go away again. He'd seen the woman who'd once been the love of his life for the first time in years. Had witnessed a speeding vehicle take aim at her. Had seen blood-soaked boots on pavement.

None of this should be happening here.

He stepped into Rich's line of sight. "Where is everybody?"

"They went with Seth. A couple of local cops took him up the road a little ways, around the curve. Probably have him sitting in a patrol car. He was pretty…you know."

Belligerent? Desperate? Scared? When they'd lost Fitz, Seth had been one of the worst wounded, nearly bleeding out from shrapnel to the neck. His fight, his determination, his will to live…everything had centered on Angie.

And now she was gone.

Jason tensed, his knee and shoulder protesting with another reminder of the ways life didn't always make sense. As he stood beside Rich, he studied the driveway leading to the back of the fire station. Seth was going to need them all, but he had no idea what to say. If they were facing armed terrorists, he could take them down. A bomb factory? Been there, done that.

But a buddy who'd lost his wife?

He hadn't felt this inept even in basic training. There weren't courses for how to comfort a guy whose wife was dead. A wife who had been killed in a hit-and-run ten miles from home with an envelope full of meth in her hand.

Rich pounded the side of his fist against the truck. "I feel useless standing here. I'd rather be hunting the guy who did this, bringing him in so he can face what he's done."

"Same."

"Lisa's with him. She'll know what Seth needs."

Lisa Fitzgerald would definitely do a better job than any of the guys would. When they'd returned from Iraq and Lisa had come to meet them, Jason had tried to offer sympathy to Fitz's wife. He'd watched her husband die. He owed her.

But he'd blown it. Had stammered a few clichés that had made her soak his shoulder with tears.

"I think—" Rich's words dropped as a figure stepped around the back of the truck.

Jason's muscles tensed, his fingers reflexively reaching for the weapon he no longer carried. People melting out of the darkness never meant anything good.

But as the shadow drew closer, the tension eased.

Sergeant First Class Tony Augustus lowered a soda can from his mouth, casting a guilty look at Jason.

"Caesar." The nickname had been bestowed on Tony by a drill sergeant who'd called him *Caesar Augustus*. "You let your wife catch you downing caffeine, she'll come after you. Then she'll come after us for not stopping you." After the incident that killed Fitz, the men had reacted in different ways. Caesar's post-traumatic stress had nearly incapacitated him and, in an effort to curb his anxiety, his wife, Caroline, had talked him into cutting his caffeine intake.

"Yeah, well…" Caesar scrubbed his hand across his closely cropped dark hair. "Tension's thick and I just needed…something."

Jason could sympathize with the need for *something*. He'd found *something* at the bottom of a bottle after *the incident*, but while it had bought him temporary freedom from the pain, it had left him helpless to fight his thoughts when the nothingness wore off. Not only did he relive Fitz's death and his own injuries, but he was thrown back to life in Mountain Springs before he took an oath to serve his country, to the *what might have beens* he'd left behind.

A few moments of oblivion weren't worth the aftermath.

Rich thumped his fist lightly against the side of his truck, a rhythmic beat that was almost reassuring. A drummer when he was in high school, he was always tapping a rhythm. The habit had led to a lot of late-night impromptu bad karaoke sessions. His engagement to his fiancée, Amber Ransom, was a few days old. He was probably internalizing all of Seth's reactions, knowing he'd do the same. He needed time. They all needed time.

Caesar leaned back against the truck. "Two cops were out front, talking earlier." He tipped his head to the sky. "They're looking at Seth." He addressed the stars. "Not sure they're wrong."

Wait a second. "You don't think…"

"Stranger things have happened after guys have seen the things we've seen." Dropping his chin, Caesar pinned Jason with a hard gaze. "Don't tell me your thoughts haven't whacked out on you before."

Jason's jaw tightened. He'd had memories he wished he could erase, nightmares he'd give anything to stop…but violence? No.

Caesar shoved off of the truck and stared at the front of the fire station. "It's not important."

But it probably was. While a couple of guys had talked to the chaplain when they'd come home, most had opted out. A diagnosis of post-traumatic stress could wreck careers, so they buried the pain deep.

Or they blew up.

"What's not important?" A familiar female voice drifted around the truck, followed by a tall, trim woman with blond hair and green eyes that held the weight of the world.

Lisa Fitzgerald.

"Nothing." Jason let her pull him into a quick hug. Then she drew him away from Caesar to the front of the vehicle.

If she was seeking comfort, she was in the wrong place.

Instead, she kept her hand on his arm, her expression speaking fear more than pain.

"What's wrong?"

"It's Crystal."

"Palmer's wife?" Jason leaned around her.

A small knot of people had gathered while he'd been talking to Caesar, but he couldn't see Drew or Crystal. "Where are they?"

"He called about five minutes ago."

"Okay…" With a gut-wrenching dread, he knew nothing good was coming.

"She had an asthma attack and…" Tears threatened to spill from Lisa's eyes.

Jason stared across the small distance at their incomplete group. Lisa didn't need to say any more.

Crystal Palmer was dead.

There was no way this was a coincidence. Someone was targeting his team.

Which meant Erin could be next.

Erin climbed onto the brush truck and inspected the handrail she'd been polishing when Jason interrupted her. It was tough to tell where she'd stopped and, honestly, she was too tired to care. As the sun brought a different light to the windows in the huge doors, she was glad to see the single most horrible night of her life end.

Chief Kelliher had released her hours ago, but she'd waited for the techs outside to pack and leave, just in case. More than once, she'd started to walk out the front door to offer condolences to Jason and the members of his team who'd stood tightly clustered near the road, but she'd stopped herself every time. It would likely be an intrusion, a distraction. They needed one another, not her.

Footsteps echoed in the hallway. It was a little bit early for Chief Kelliher, but he'd likely driven half the night to get back from the conference in Nashville and had probably come straight to the station.

But, for the second time, the man who walked around the truck wasn't who she'd expected.

With a heavy sigh that served to weigh her down more, Erin turned her eyes to the ceiling. "Jason." When she trusted herself enough to look at him, he'd stopped a few feet away. The lines around his eyes were deeper than they'd been earlier, fatigue drawing deep circles underneath.

One eyebrow arched but settled again, and his expression darkened. "I wouldn't have bothered you if I didn't think it was important."

"What else could possibly—"

"Erin."

The heavy command in his tone stopped the flow of her tirade.

Jason caught her gaze in a way he hadn't in years…and his expression was anything but friendly. It held a hint of something she'd never seen before, something that swept chills across her skin.

With an underlying authority she'd never heard before, he broke the silence. "I think you're in danger."

She was in danger?

Sure she was.

The single threat Erin saw was the one standing ten feet from her. He was the one person alive who could wreck her entire world by making her want things she could never have.

Ignoring the twinge in her chest that remembered how it used to be, Erin jumped off the truck but kept her distance from the man she'd once trusted above all others. Their story was in the past. And while tonight had been horrifying, his assertion she was in danger made her think Jason was a couple of matches short of a full box. If he was referring to the text, it had nothing to do with her. It had been a decoy, a way for a killer to draw Angie Daniels to her death.

"Okay, Jason. Whatever game you're playing, I'm leaving the field." Erin dropped the rag into a bucket and reached for the handle. She should go home anyway. Her father would be texting again soon, trying to track her down. His demands were pretty much the extent of what she could deal with this morning. "It's been a long night. I want to go home and sleep. Nothing else. Please, just go."

Not wanting to risk a brush past him in the narrow space between the trucks, Erin turned and headed for the back of the ladder truck to circle around to the front of the building. It might make her seem like a coward, but no way did she want to risk contact with him, not the way her brain kept pinging back into the past every time she looked at him and definitely not when he was talking as though reality was no longer a friend of his. She'd spent eight years mending her broken heart, and the roller coaster of the past seven hours had left her spent and defenseless.

Footsteps and his hand on her bicep stopped her. "You know me well enough to know this isn't a game."

Erin jerked her arm from his grasp and kept walking, the first zip of fear running across her skin. She may have been moved to protect his emotions last night, but the truth was she didn't know this Jason at all. People changed. Circumstances shaped everyone. For all she knew of this stranger, he was behind every crazy thing happening in the small town.

She had to get outside, call Wyatt, do something to get away from—

"Another wife of a guy on my team died this morning. Early. Not too long after Angie. Asthma attack."

Erin's footsteps dragged to a stop and the bucket hung limp in her hands. She'd heard the call for EMS on the county's dispatch, but she'd been so involved with what was happening in front of her, she hadn't processed it. The station in Fairview, right outside of Camp McGee, had responded. Unlike Angie's murder, which would be all over the place as soon as the story worked its way to the news stations in Asheville, there was no way Jason would have any clue about the other death unless someone close to the deceased had told him.

Her jaw tightened. If someone wanted to hurt her, they'd missed their chance last night, because the driver of the car had a clear shot and waved off. "This has nothing to do with me."

"Both of us know two spouses of men on my team dying at the same time would be one of the craziest coincidences in the world. And Angie's death was no accident. Neither was someone trying to link you to it." Jason stepped close enough for Erin to feel the warmth of his presence against her back. She dug her teeth into her lower lip as the pain of losing him swept her, as fresh as if he'd left yesterday. "Problem is, there's more. I talked to my former chain of command about an hour ago. Late yesterday evening, my buddy Cole Dawson's ex-wife was found dead in Roanoke, Virginia. Her roommate came home from work and she was on the couch with her car running in the garage. They were thinking accident or suicide, but... Three spouses in one day? From the same team?" His hand was warm on her shoulder as he turned her to face him. "A team whose last successful mission involved taking out some high-value targets that might cause someone to want revenge?"

Last *successful* mission? Erin's thoughts tripped over the word, then stuck on what he was trying to tell her. It couldn't be real. Life wasn't as bizarre as the movies. "You can't be serious. You sound ridiculous. That's some old Bruce Willis action movie kind of stuff. The bad guys don't get revenge the way you're saying, not on individuals. They come after whole countries. Big targets to make a statement, not families." He was insane. Out of his head. Nobody came to Mountain Springs to commit murder.

Except she'd seen the carnage with her own eyes a few hours earlier.

Still, there was no way. She rolled the handle of the bucket between two fingers and refused to meet his eyes. "Even if it was true, I'm your ex. Anybody trying to get revenge couldn't care less about someone who means nothing to you."

Everything about Jason froze. He looked as though she'd slapped him and he didn't know how to handle the blow. But then he jerked his head to the side and continued as though the pause never happened. "You're forgetting Cole's ex. The Dawsons got divorced before we did. Cole never remarried. He always said Tracy was it for him, the same way…" Jason dropped his hand from her arm. "Somehow, some way, somebody with a grudge found Tracy. And Angie and Crystal. In two different cities. And until somebody figures out how they got their intel, I can't promise whoever this is doesn't know about you too."

This was too much. Between Angie's death and Jason's reappearance…

Erin tried to read him, to find something familiar in the man in front of her, but all she could see was a hardness around the edges that hadn't existed before. "What happened to you overseas?" It had to have been something, because nothing else could explain the things he was saying. The story simply couldn't be real.

His head dipped to one side, confusion clouding his gaze. "What?"

"You walk with a limp. Not much of one, but enough. I noticed it earlier. And this? This story you're spinning?" When his mouth opened to say more, she backed farther away and dug deep for the strength to walk away, even as her heart wanted to reach out to him. "I'm about to grab my truck keys out of the office. You're going to walk out ahead of me without saying another word. Because if you don't, I'm having Wyatt come back to handle you and your crazy talk. Don't speak to me again." *Because I don't have what it takes to remember why it all went wrong in the first place.*

When she turned, he didn't follow. Jason had always been the pragmatic one, the level-headed one, while she'd been the one wanting to run away and do crazy things like eloping in South Carolina. To think a mind as solid and steady as his had cracked...

Her throat ached. She'd heard about men coming home broken, different... She'd simply never imagined it would happen to Jason. He'd always been the strongest man she knew.

Without pausing, she dropped the bucket next to the row of wall lockers and swept into the office, snatching her keys from the corner of the desk and holding them so tightly they dug into her palms. If he didn't leave as she'd asked, she'd…she'd…

Cry. His brokenness would break her.

But his footsteps didn't pause as he headed up the hall. The outside door opened and shut softly and the building fell silent.

Erin dropped her chin to her chest and stared at the scuffed toes of her black boots, feeling as though her spine couldn't support her any longer. Last night had been too long, too much of a breakneck ride down the mountain at top speed. She couldn't do any more. And if she didn't get out of this building in the next ten seconds, she was going to fall to pieces.

Maybe she'd make the drive home slowly with the windows down. Maybe last night would blow away somewhere into the fall mountain mist.

When she broke through the door into the early morning light, she scanned the parking lot, half expecting to see Jason waiting.

The small front lot was empty.

She'd deny until her last breath that his departure left her with a hint of disappointment.

It was for the best. He was gone. Hopefully for good, the way he should have been when their divorce was final.

Jerking open the door to the Bronco, Erin climbed in and reached for the seat belt as she angled her foot toward the brake. Her heel rolled on something and an all-too-familiar sound paralyzed her, cold terror icing her movements and driving the world into slow motion.

No. There was no way. None. She had to be dreaming. Or hallucinating.

Tilting her head, she looked at her foot, throat dry, head pounding…

And found a rattlesnake beneath the heel of her boot.

FOUR

Jason sat in his pickup and kneaded the steering wheel, the leather warming rapidly beneath his palms. Erin could kick him out of the fire station, but the roads were still public and she couldn't stop him from following her home. She might not realize how dangerous the situation was, but he did. He'd seen what terror cells with vengeance on their minds could do. Had seen havoc the general public knew nothing about. Had both witnessed and experienced pain on an exponential scale.

He wasn't going to let whoever was out for blood lay one cold finger on Erin. If she was in danger, it was his fault for dragging her into it. It was his responsibility to make sure she didn't suffer because of him.

But for one brief moment, as the rising sun overtook one of the most emotionally agonizing nights of his life, her words found their mark. Erin truly believed he'd lost his mind.

Her expression spoke of her certainty. She'd once looked at him as though he was her hero, as though he could protect her from anything. Her accusations highlighted the fact they no longer knew one another at all.

Or did she still know him all too well?

His life hadn't been an easy one. At fifteen, he'd wandered out of his bedroom on a Thursday morning to an empty rental house and fifty bucks in the middle of the table. His parents never made contact again other than to sign off on his emancipation papers after the lawyer tracked them down. So when Erin had wanted to keep their marriage hidden... Of course it had cut. Deeper than he'd initially wanted to admit.

And only a few hours earlier, he'd been confronted with Caesar's confession to thoughts of violence, had even had a smug moment where he'd congratulated himself on never having them.

But what if he had? What if Erin was right and his past had spiraled into some sort of post-deployment paranoia?

No. He knew Angie was dead. His whole team had received the news about Crystal. And both he and Rich had spoken to Captain Miller and been informed about Tracy Dawson. This wasn't a figment of his imagination. This was very real.

Someone was out to make his team pay. And in Angie's case, it was particularly brutal.

The muscles in his knee twitched, and his shoulder joined in with a sympathetic twinge of its own. The ache was always there, on the periphery, but he'd learned to ignore it. Not this morning. The longer it took Erin to pull away from the fire station, the tenser his body grew and the more pain ran through newly healed scars.

She should have driven away by now. Jason knew she'd grabbed her keys before he walked out the door. He'd heard them rattle. She should have left the building close behind him.

His gut burned. This wasn't right. Had someone else been in the building? Had he missed the biggest threat of all?

Without considering the consequences, Jason shoved the door of the truck open and slipped to the edge of the brick building, peering toward the front door.

Erin's Bronco sat where he'd last seen it, facing away from him. But the driver's-side door hung open and Erin's figure sat straight and stiff in the front seat, cast in silhouette by the morning light filtering through the windshield.

Why wasn't she moving?

There hadn't been a rifle shot, so there was no way a sniper had hit her. He'd have seen someone fleeing the parking lot. There was no way…

Unless someone had been waiting for her in the Bronco.

Open space stood between the vehicle and his concealed position. If he moved in, he was going to have to move fast and pray no one in the vicinity saw him coming.

Anticipation pumping like liquid fire through his veins, Jason breathed in and out slowly. He prepared to go hand-to-hand and raced for the car, scanning the windows as he went, seeing no one but Erin.

If she was sitting there processing the events of the night and he raced toward her, this wild-goose chase would solidify her thoughts about his sanity.

Jason staggered to a halt beside the car, his foot sliding on loose gravel. He regained his balance as he reached the door.

Erin sat alone, staring at her feet. Her face was the kind of white he'd only seen on people who were already beyond help. Her eyes were wide. Her fingers dug into her thigh so tightly, they were bound to be causing her pain.

He'd heard of terror before, had felt it himself, but never to the degree it rolled off Erin now. "Erin?" Jason struggled to keep his voice low, and he reached out to touch her shoulder.

She whimpered, the sound small and pitiful. Then the lines of her face tensed impossibly tighter.

A rustling drifted from the floorboard of the truck, and Jason's own muscles seized as he followed her line of sight to her feet.

The heel of Erin's boot had pinned a rattlesnake behind the head. The creature writhed and rattled, trying to break free so it could strike.

Jason backed an instinctive step away from the threat, his hand going to his chin, his fingers digging into his jaw. Nothing in the world scared Erin more than a snake. She'd faced burning buildings, had worked in spaces small enough to make normal people hyperventilate and had performed field medicine on the kinds of injuries that would buckle the knees of grown men. But snakes? Being pinned in with a rattler had to be the pinnacle of her nightmares.

Snakes weren't his favorite either. The

wriggling creature beneath Erin's boot made him want to run for safety himself. In Ranger School, they'd made camp at Fort Benning and one of the guys had been bitten on the hand while gathering wood for a fire. The symptoms were nearly instantaneous and the pain…

Jason swallowed hard. Erin should not have to go through this. Shoving aside his own instincts, he eased closer and rested one hand on her shoulder and one on the hand she was digging into her thigh. "I've got you." He kept his voice low and packed it with as much reassurance as he could muster.

Her gaze flicked to his as though she finally realized he was there. The abject terror in her eyes nailed him to the ground. He'd fix this. He had to.

"I'll get you out of here. Hang with me, ET." The old nickname, one he hadn't spoken in half a decade, was thick and awkward on his tongue, but her shoulder relaxed slightly beneath his fingers as she released the breath she'd been holding.

For once, he must be doing something right.

Tightening his fingers around hers, Jason steeled himself to study the snake. The heel of her boot had landed perfectly about two inches behind the rattler's head, pinning him into immobility. If she'd been trying, she couldn't have hit him at a better spot to protect herself. But the way the creature was thrashing, it could roll free at any second, and those beasts could strike faster than Erin could get clear.

If she so much as twitched...

"I need you to stay really, really still."

"No worries there." Her voice was reed thin, but at least she was listening.

Gnawing on the inside of his cheek, Jason rapidly ran through the possibilities. Unless things had changed, Erin kept a .38 Ruger revolver in the glove compartment of the Bronco, but there was no way he could shoot the snake without risking Erin's foot. Even then, the thing could still strike after it was dead.

She couldn't climb out fast enough on her own, and pulling her out would be a tricky proposition. If her foot got hung on the brake pedal or if they were one hair of a second too slow, the snake would have her by the foot.

He could call for help, but he couldn't guarantee it would arrive fast enough. Erin's hold on the snake was too tenuous, and she was so tense she was bound to fatigue fast.

Three terrible options.

The snake rattled again, and Jason studied

the length of the serpent from its rattle and back to Erin's foot.

Wait.

"Those boots. Leather?" *Oh please, let them be leather.*

She nodded once.

"They go above your ankle?"

Another nod.

Maybe he could pull her out fast enough to keep a strike out of range of her calf. But it would take her cooperation and all the strength he had in his still-healing knee and shoulder.

Jason counted to five to steady himself, then arranged his face into an expression he hoped was calm and convincing. "I'm getting you out of here. You ready?"

"Been ready." The words came through a clenched jaw. Boy, he hoped she was.

"Okay. You cannot move your foot until I say so. But I need you to put your arms around my neck and hang on."

She made a low sound in her throat but didn't say anything. Slowly, she relaxed her arms and let Jason guide her hands around his neck, though her leg stayed stiff. Her muscles had to be aching.

"I'm counting to three and then I'm diving backward. You're going with me. You ready?"

"No, but count anyway."

Erin Taylor was still the bravest woman he knew. When this was over, he'd hug her whether she liked it or not.

"One…"

Her hold around his neck tightened.

"Two…" Jason bent his knees and tried not to think about the asphalt drive and how it wasn't going to cushion his fall.

"Three!"

Erin launched sideways into his chest and Jason propelled them backward. He landed flat on his back as Erin's weight landed on his chest and crushed his shoulder into the ground. The pain drove white light through him, dulling his hearing and tingeing the edges of the world with black. There was a brief flash of his past self, staring at his own blood on his hands as Fitz screamed nearby.

Jason heaved in air. It wasn't real. Erin was real. The snake was real. The rest was history.

By the time he'd gathered his senses, Erin had rolled away and lay on her back, hyperventilating and staring blankly at the sky.

Kicking the door shut so the snake couldn't make an exit, Jason rolled onto his side and scanned Erin's face, running his fingers along the back of her head, feeling for bumps or blood.

Her eyes locked onto his and her breathing slowed.

There was a shift in the air, and Jason couldn't move. He was acutely aware of the softness of her hair between his fingers, of the light green around the brown in her eyes, of the way he hovered over her now the same way he had the first time he'd kissed her years ago.

He could kiss her again, right now.

But before he could move, Erin jerked her head, her hair slipping through his fingers as she rolled onto her side, shutting him out. She shoved to her hands and knees, then stood shakily, bracing against the side of the building with her back to him.

Jason rolled onto his back and sat up, watching her. Every instinct drove him to help, but he'd seen the look in her eyes before she turned away. She'd shake him off.

And it would be the right thing to do.

Tires rolled on concrete and a red pickup with the Mountain Springs VFD logo emblazoned on the side eased to a stop behind Erin's Bronco.

The fire chief.

Jason stood, unsure how to proceed. He'd saved Erin's life, but then... Then he'd almost trashed it all over again.

As the older man climbed from the vehicle and headed toward Erin, Jason distanced himself even more, no longer certain if the greatest danger to them both was from the outside…or from him.

Through the thinning autumn leaves, the two-story white-painted house stood silent at the edge of a large meadow. It was a little more worn than Jason's memory gave it credit for, and the grass could use a good pass with a mower, but nothing else had changed. Majestic white oaks still overshadowed the house, their branches brushing the black shingled roof. The two-story red barn still stood out back, its top floor holding one of the most sacred spaces he'd ever been privileged to enter, one full of memories and peace.

Too bad the peace was a big fat lie.

Jason leaned back against his truck, crossed his arms and studied the house, very much aware that if Erin spotted him she'd call Wyatt and have him arrested for stalking.

She had no idea he'd already talked to Wyatt and gotten his approval to keep an eye on her. Wyatt had sworn him to secrecy, but his willingness to let Jason get involved said that even he believed evidence suggested Erin was in danger. The snake had proved it.

Chief Kelliher had called a buddy of his to remove the snake from Erin's car, and Jason had stayed on the periphery, trying not to call attention to his presence, while they concluded the reptile had slithered inside the vehicle searching for warmth.

Jason and Wyatt disagreed. The snake was no cold-blooded critter trying to find shelter. Reptiles hid in warm engine compartments, not cold interiors. Besides, Jason had helped restore the Bronco. There wasn't a space anywhere for a snake to wriggle in.

Someone had deliberately placed it there.

So when Erin had insisted she could drive herself home, Jason had followed at a discreet distance, filling Wyatt in as he drove. Whether she believed it or not, she was a target. He had no doubt. His team still had thirteen more days of leave, and Jason planned to devote his time to ensuring no one laid a finger on her.

Erin was in trouble because of him, because he'd impulsively married her. Because with her as his beneficiary, his insurance paperwork left a trail straight to her. The fragile links he'd left in place had led a killer straight to her, and it was Jason's responsibility to make sure whoever was wreaking havoc on his team didn't succeed in harming her.

If only he could protect her from her father as easily. Jason's fists dug into the backs of his arms. There was no telling what was going on inside the house. Even after the drama with the snake, Erin had been frantic to get home.

Maybe over the past few years Kevin Taylor had mellowed and come to appreciate the daughter who had sacrificed more for him than he would ever know. Maybe her hurry this morning had been born out of concern rather than fear. That had been Jason's prayer.

"Are you kidding me?" Erin's rough whisper broke the silence as she appeared at the end of the driveway about twenty feet from his position, stalking toward him with the exact fury he'd imagined in her only a moment earlier.

Jason's body tensed, but he held his place. He'd been too deep in his own head and had let himself get caught. Nothing to do about it now but pray he was wrong about her calling the police.

As she got closer, she slowed to a walk. "Those gaps in the trees work both ways, you know. I saw you the minute I turned into the driveway. You're terrible at hiding." She crossed her arms and leveled a glare on him. "This has gone far enough. I'm calling Wyatt."

"Go ahead." Jason dropped his arms to his sides and squared off against the woman who used to be his entire world.

She searched his face for a moment before her gaze lost its intensity. "You already talked to him."

Jason nodded once.

"Why?" It was hard to tell if the tone in her voice was defeat or sheer weariness, but since she wasn't turning on her heel and walking away, Jason took it as a sign to keep talking.

"He's worried about you, same as I am. He thought someone keeping an eye on you until we figure out what's going on might be a good thing."

"Why is it you think this involves me?" She dropped her arms to her sides and walked closer, leaning her hip against the front of the pickup. "You know what? It doesn't matter. You and Wyatt, you're both persistent, and neither of you is going to back off."

She was right about that. There was no need to tell her that, while their marriage had imploded, he'd never severed his friendship with her cousin. Wyatt had figured letting her know might cause her too much pain.

"If I can ask one question—how is it you happen to be around when all of this chaos breaks loose?"

It was a question, not an accusation. If he were standing in her shoes, he'd be asking the same thing.

"I told you earlier. Some of the guys from my unit got orders to McGee." The line sounded canned, but it was the best he could do without delving into the incident that had decimated his fire team.

"So you're here for a while."

"Once they catch the guys doing this, you won't even know I'm nearby. You'll be safe from me."

A sad smile tipped the corner of her mouth. "Was I ever not safe with you?" She shook her head and turned to stare at the house through the trees. "You never made me feel anything else."

Unlike her father. Wyatt had kept Jason updated over the past few years. Nothing had changed since he left. Even this morning's conversation had reinforced that every member of Wyatt's family had tried to talk to her, but Erin couldn't see what her own father was doing to her.

"She'll never be free of him if she can't see the truth, Jase. You and I both know Kevin Taylor was never a good man. He was a selfish beast before my aunt Kara died, and he's gotten worse. He uses his medical condition

to keep Erin tied to him, convinced it's her lot in life. So, yeah, nothing's changed. If anything, it's gotten worse. The one thing she won't give up is the fire department, and she's held back there because she can't get away from him long enough to get the training she needs to move up."

For the hundredth time in twelve hours, Jason's stomach threatened to revolt. He'd prayed and hoped for years that things would be different, that Erin would learn the truth of who she was and get free of her father's lies, maybe even find someone to love her the way she deserved.

Although the idea of her with someone else had never settled well with him and had even kept him awake more than a few nights.

One of the reasons he'd married her had been to get her out of that house. But when her father had his stroke, Erin had refused to reveal their marriage. Had refused to move out no matter how hard Jason had tried to make her see the truth.

Until it tore them apart. Jason had grown tired of feeling as though he was sneaking around with his own wife, of feeling as though she was ashamed to be seen with him, and had worn himself out trying to find a decent job in a tiny town. He'd joined the military and asked her to come away with him.

The move had backfired monumentally. Divorce papers when he came out of basic proved it.

"The problem is, you hurt a lot of people when you took off." It was as though Erin could read his thoughts and jumped right into the internal conversation, totally uninvited.

"I know." This conversation had been coming for years. In the back of his mind, Jason had always known the way he left without looking back was wrong. "I don't have any excuses you'd want to hear. And all I can do is apologize."

Her expression softened a bit, but there was still an unyielding hardness around the edges. She wasn't going to let him off the hook that easily. "Wyatt's parents took it hard. It would be great if you found a way to swing by their house and tell them."

Jason winced. Clearly, she didn't want to talk about them.

But she was also right. He owed Wyatt's parents even more. While he'd stayed in touch with Wyatt sporadically, he hadn't been able to face Wyatt's parents. When Jason's own parents had abandoned him at fifteen, the Stephens family had taken him in until he could work through the court system to gain emancipation at sixteen. Cade and Deanna Stephens had treated him like their second son and Wyatt had become more than his best friend. He'd become a brother. The Stephenses' home had been where Jason had gotten to know Erin as more than a tagalong. It was the Stephenses' barn where they'd first started restoring Erin's Bronco, and where he'd first kissed her. It had been Wyatt who helped them elope, although they'd never told his parents.

Jason had abandoned them all.

At least they'd probably felt that way. He'd wanted nothing more than to be married to Erin, and then he was and she'd wanted to keep it a secret. For a while, he'd understood. Her father hated him, and with his stroke coming immediately after the accident, it made sense not to upset him. But as the first year passed and they entered the second, as Erin started community college and Jason tried to find a job to prove he could support her, it had all grown too huge. They'd needed money. They'd needed time together.

"You know what?" Erin's voice drew Jason out of his thoughts.

He'd been quiet too long, lost in his own head again.

When he looked over at her, she'd straightened and was turning to walk away. "It's been a very long, very surreal, very ugly night, and all I want to do is go to bed. Stay out here, don't stay out here, whatever. But please…" She rubbed at her temple as though a headache was lodged there. "Don't let my dad see you. I can't deal with that on top of everything else." With a half-hearted wave, she turned and walked away, disappearing into the trees along the driveway before Jason could find the words to make her stay.

FIVE

Shutting the front door behind her, Erin dropped her duffel bag on the kitchen table and leaned heavily on the back of a ladder-back chair. She was done. Done with death and insanity and the past...and snakes.

Nausea had rolled through her in waves for the entire drive home. So far, she'd managed to keep from losing anything left of last night's dinner, and she wanted to keep it that way. Catching a glimpse of Jason following her as she'd pulled into her driveway hadn't helped matters. If she were more herself and not so destroyed by the events of the night, she'd have had a lot more to say to him, things that included him never coming within a hundred feet of her again.

As it was, she was too exhausted to fight him. And if Wyatt truly was approving this lunatic idea of Jason following her around, she'd lose the battle anyway. She was definitely too brain-dead to take them both on.

If she could crawl into bed and pull the covers over her head for a few hours, surely things would be better when she awoke.

They couldn't get much worse.

"'Bout time you got home." From the den, the recliner slammed shut, and the hardwood floors creaked as her father lumbered to the kitchen door, moving a little slower than usual. His graying hair was rumpled as though she'd awakened him. He was wearing his trademark khakis and blue mechanic's shirt, dressed for work.

Although he never actually went.

"I had a rough night." Why bother to say anything more? He already knew there'd been some "excitement" at the station. If she told the whole story about Angie Daniels, he'd ask why Erin hadn't been able to save her. Forget telling him she'd nearly been a rattler's breakfast. He'd ask when she was going to "man up" and realize snakes were a part of life in the mountains. He would be right on all counts, but her brain was toast and discussion wasn't an option.

"You could've let me know you'd be running late. I've been texting you." The words slurred slightly and his eyes were half-closed, as though he'd been deep asleep in front of the morning talk shows and hadn't quite sloughed off the heaviness. "Can't get myself breakfast now, can I?"

Ever since they'd found out her father had type 2 diabetes, he'd needed Erin to help him survive. She had just begun to assert her independence in high school when the diagnosis came. Softball, cheer... Kevin Taylor had made his daughter surrender almost everything to take care of him. Erin had traded romance novels for cookbooks and medical studies, made sure he had healthy meals and kept his prescriptions filled and at the ready.

None of it had mattered. In the end, Erin had nearly killed him.

The stroke was her fault. If she hadn't taken off with Jason, hadn't insisted on taking the Camaro in some sort of celebratory joyride, hadn't let herself get injured... If that night had never happened, then the stroke that robbed her father of the full strength of his left arm never would have happened. He'd still be working and she wouldn't have to be protecting him from himself. Things would be so much different if she hadn't screwed up. She destroyed everything she touched.

This morning was a prime example. She should have called and asked Uncle Joe to check on him. If he didn't eat by eight, his blood sugar would pay the price. And if he saw Jason hanging around the house?

There was no telling how high that price would be.

Rest wasn't coming anytime soon. "Did you really wait for me to get home to eat, Dad? It's after ten. You know you have to eat or your sugar—"

"I dug around in the pantry and found myself something to take the edge off, no thanks to you, too busy out running the roads or something to make sure I'm fed and healthy. You'll be sorry if I wind up in the ER again."

The steady throbbing that had set up camp behind her right eye during her conversation with Jason pulsed harder. There were hard-boiled eggs already peeled in the refrigerator. Fruit cut and bagged in serving-sized portions. Whole wheat bagels sitting right beside the toaster. Did he think stuff just appeared?

She counted to ten. He was right. The least she could have done was texted him to remind him she'd left snacks for him. "Well, if it happens again, there's food in the fridge all ready for you." Erin swiped her duffel off the table and headed for her room. Maybe she could catch a nap before she headed out to cut the grass. He'd been complaining about it for the past few days and was sure to mention it again if she hung around too long, especially since he was extra cranky this morning. This was what she deserved for coming home late. "What did you eat?"

"Swiss cake rolls and a Pepsi."

"What?" She whirled on him. "Tell me you're kidding." While Erin was practically addicted to those things at the firehouse, she made sure never to leave them at home. It made her a hypocrite maybe, but it was her comfort food, the one thing she wouldn't give up. Some firefighters drank away what they saw on the job. She fed her troubles sugar and caffeine, and the end result worked just as well.

"Nope. Found them in the back of the pantry. You hiding them from me?"

"Definitely not." She'd never brought those into the house, but maybe, if they were in the back, they were old? Some she'd forgotten? A misstep like he implied made her incredibly careless or incredibly stupid.

She couldn't lecture her father, not when she'd left him the ammo to do damage to himself. Besides, there wasn't enough reserve left in her to hold her tongue if she got started, and the last thing either of them needed was for him to lose his temper and spike his blood pressure. "Did you check your blood sugar today? Take your insulin?" *Did you do anything to take care of yourself?*

"I'm not a child, Erin Joanna. Don't talk to me like I am." Although he'd probably intended the words to come out on a shout, they came out as more of a loud whisper.

Erin let her bag fall to the faded yellow linoleum floor as she took a step closer to her father. "Dad?" Her practiced eye put the pieces together. Drooping eyelids. Slurred speech. And increasing difficulty breathing.

Jerking out the kitchen chair, she shoved her father down by the shoulder and reached for her phone. "Dad." The word almost choked her. "I think you're having another stroke."

Erin paced the small curtained space in the emergency room. When she was on the job, she hardly noticed the sharp scent of antiseptic or the stale food odor drifting through the halls of a hospital, but today... With her adrenaline crashing and her stomach empty and already twisted with anxiety, the smell was almost more than she could handle.

The ambulance had whisked her father in and she'd followed with Jason, who'd appeared as soon as her father was loaded into the ambulance and offered to drive her. She'd been too frazzled and scared to turn him down, and she had no idea where he was now that she'd been escorted back into the ER.

A nurse wearing gray scrubs had promised to bring news as soon as they were done running a battery of tests to determine if this was another stroke.

A stroke she could have prevented.

She'd known she should have called Joe. Instead, she'd left her father to worry about her and to fend for himself.

How could she have been so careless? Let him get his hands on something that could kill him?

This was all her fault. And if her father died, she'd have to live with her mistake for the rest of her life.

Dropping onto a blue plastic chair, she buried her face in her hands. Maybe she should leave the fire department and take a regular nine to five somewhere so she could be home with him more. But at night he was asleep and didn't need her. If she was gone all day and he was on his own? She didn't even want to think about how that would work.

And if she left the fire department and took a different job, she could lose the grant she'd counted on for the past eight years. Wyatt had helped her apply. A foundation gave her a few hundred dollars every month because she was a firefighter caring for an ailing parent. Without the boost, she'd have had to take on an extra job, forcing her to be home even less.

But the grant was only for firefighters. If she lost the money, they could lose everything.

The weight on her shoulders was too heavy. The burden of caring for her father, of making sure there was food in the pantry and the bills were paid… It was more than she could handle. She was exhausted, couldn't remember the last time she'd truly slept. Could barely remember the last time she'd eaten.

Once they figured out what was wrong with her dad and she got some good food and quality rest, then she'd be able to pick up her life and carry it again. She had to. There was no one else to take her place.

A light tap on the wall lifted her head, and a young nurse stepped into the overly lit space. She wore navy blue pants and a scrub top covered in superheroes. Her dark hair waved tight to her head, and her deep brown eyes were heavy with compassion. "Doing okay?"

Erin offered a weak nod. No use dumping her problems on an ER nurse who likely had more than enough stress and exhaustion of her own.

"Listen, it's going to be about an hour before your father is brought back in. There's someone asking about him in the lobby if you want to go out for a bit. He's stable right now, and we'll have some better answers for you soon." She lifted a slight smile. "Believe it or not, the cafeteria food here isn't half-bad and you look like you could use some fuel. I recommend the breakfast burrito."

It was too much information at once. Erin had to run through it all slowly in her head to get everything straight. The ache in her gut said she needed food first, but someone was in the lobby asking about her father? Who? It couldn't be Jason. Surely he was long gone rather than hanging around in the same building as her father. He wasn't exactly known for hanging around.

Her father didn't really have any friends who'd come around either. He didn't even go to church. His socialization was TV and occasionally hanging around at the auto body shop where he used to work.

No way Joe or any of his employees even knew what was going on, let alone had the time to leave work to come here.

Guess she'd better see who was asking

about her dad first, then move on to food. Hopefully it wouldn't take long. Her knees were wobbling from hunger and exhaustion.

At the entrance, the nurse stepped aside and gave Erin directions to the waiting area, then slipped into the next room with a cheery *hello*.

Erin shoved through the swinging double doors at the end of the hallway and found Jason standing a few feet away. The lines around his eyes said he was as done with this day as she was. He'd endured so much more than she had, and yet…he was here?

Erin's steps slowed. He shouldn't be. Not only would her father somehow *know* he was hanging around, the guy simply wasn't known for sticking around when the going got tough.

At least he hadn't in their marriage.

When he spotted her, he lifted a white paper bag. "Bacon, egg and cheese sandwich? They had them in the cafeteria."

He remembered. When she'd been on duty at the fire station during their marriage, he would stop on his way to his early class in the morning with a bacon, egg and cheese sandwich from the small grill at the gas station on the outside of town.

She hadn't eaten one since he'd left.

With the salty scent of bacon heading straight for her stomach, Erin kept her eyes on her ex-husband as she gingerly took the bag, working hard not to brush his fingers. Exhaustion and shock made the whole scene feel like one of the dreams she frequently had, the ones where he'd come back for her. Every time, she woke up in almost physical pain to find that nothing had changed.

"How's your dad?" Jason stepped aside and held out his arm toward a small glassed-in room containing some vending machines and a couple of plastic tables, breaking the spell.

"I don't know." She walked into the room ahead of him and sank into a chair, then unwrapped the sandwich but didn't take a bite. Jason's presence was thick in the room, tugging at her to confide in him, but there was no good way to do so without sounding needy or nostalgic.

Jason sat across from her and shoved a hefty cup of coffee her way. She hadn't even noticed he was holding it. "Drink it. You need the caffeine."

Wrapping her hands around the paper cup, Erin let the warmth seep up her arms without taking a sip. Right now, she needed to smell it. She kept one hand on the coffee and grabbed her sandwich with the other, finishing half before she set it on the table and swigged the still-warm drink.

When she glanced at Jason over the rim of her coffee cup, he was studying her face.

Once, when she was a teenager, Erin had stared into a mirror for so long she'd almost become a stranger to herself. Those eyes in the mirror knew her deepest thoughts, her unconfessed fears and everything about her from the inside out. It had freaked her out until she'd closed her eyes to shake the shivers away.

That was how she felt with Jason. He had once known all of her dreams and plans and thoughts…but he hadn't been able to understand her.

Now this man who'd known her better than any other was a stranger. It was so hard to make her brain compute.

It was also impossible to keep from confiding in him.

"This is my fault, you know." She tore her gaze from Jason to look at the snack machine, tapping her finger on the side of the coffee cup.

"This isn't your fault. You did everything you could to make sure he was taken care of. He made a choice—"

"I didn't give him enough information. Didn't—"

"Erin." Jason said her name and it once again carried the weight of a command that turned her toward him. His jaw moved like he was going to say something else, but then his mouth set in a tight line.

"Say it."

"You have to stop taking responsibility for him. Wyatt and I talked earlier and—"

Erin slammed her palms on the table. Whatever was going on, she was already tired of their buddy-buddy behavior. Jason had reappeared twelve hours ago. Had Wyatt seriously already forgiven him and charged straight back into the friendship they used to have? "You two have been talking about me? At what point did you find the time to—"

"Ms. Taylor?"

Erin whipped her head around to find a nurse leaning in the door to the snack area. "Your father is being moved upstairs to a room if you'd like to wait for him there."

The best place to be right now was in the room when her father got there. If she wasn't, he'd have an earful waiting for her when she arrived.

Without acknowledging the man who'd apparently conspired with her cousin to solve all of her problems without her input, Erin left her breakfast on the table and followed the nurse, praying whatever news waited for her, it wouldn't derail the rest of her life.

The nurse aimed a finger down the hallway. "He'll be in room 382. I'd take you there but we're shorthanded today."

"No problem. I can find it." She'd been here enough to visit accident victims or people from church. Jogging up the hallway that led to the single staircase in this wing of the small hospital, Erin prayed her father was okay and that she'd make it to the room ahead of him. She hesitated at the elevator, fired off a quick update to Wyatt, then pocketed her phone and decided to take her usual route up the stairs. Her friend Jenna teased her about the way she ran stairs, but it was an easy way to stay in shape and to rehearse the routes in case she ever had to take them during a fire, when elevators would be off-limits. Today, with a small knot of people already waiting for the elevator, her way would likely be faster.

Halfway to the second floor, the door a level lower crashed open, and footsteps pounded up the stark concrete and metal stairs. Erin hesitated and turned toward the sound. Someone was coming fast and that meant trouble. She backed up against the wall to make way for whatever doctor or nurse was rushing up the stairs.

The figure that rounded the landing had on jeans and a shapeless gray hooded sweatshirt pulled low to cover their face. When they lifted their head, a ski mask obscured any features.

Erin's heart pounded from exertion and fear. She had to move, to get higher or get past the person who had fixed a hard gaze on her and raced up the steps toward her.

As Erin turned to bolt up the stairs away from danger, a gloved hand clamped around her wrist and jerked her backward, slinging her down the half flight of stairs she'd just climbed. Her shoulder slammed into the wall. She tried to catch her footing and missed, tumbling to the concrete below. Her cheek cracked on the concrete floor.

Pain flung stars spinning across her vision as voices echoed down the stairs from another floor.

The figure hesitated, then leaped over Erin and disappeared down the stairs.

SIX

Jason stared in the direction Erin had gone. He shouldn't let her out of his sight, but the risk of running into her father and setting off that explosion was too high. The fire blazing under his skin when Erin took responsibility for her father's actions had almost seared away the tether on his tongue. They'd been down that road a thousand times, and it always ended in a fiery crash over a cliff. She'd never see what her father was doing to her, how he was destroying her.

Or how she was letting him.

Sitting across from her under the harsh glow of fluorescent hospital lights, he'd been able to see her even more clearly than in the bay of the fire station. She was thinner, her eyes sunken. Some of the problem could be attributed to the repeated shocks of the hours before, but some of it was chronic.

He was two seconds from following her

when Wyatt rounded the corner and caught sight of Jason standing in the doorway. Erin's cousin was still wearing his uniform and looking as weary as she had. "Erin with her dad?"

"She just went upstairs."

"She texted me as I was walking in. Told me the room number." Wyatt's eyebrow arched. "You deciding how safe she is if you don't follow her?"

"Wouldn't want her dad to see me, would we?" The words were acid on Jason's tongue. After all this time, it shouldn't matter. But it did. Erin should be free. But she wasn't. "Somebody needs to talk to her."

"You think I haven't tried? Mom and Dad haven't tried? Jenna hasn't tried?"

Jason lifted his head, his forehead creasing. "Who's Jenna?"

"She moved to town right around the time you and Erin got... Around the time things ended."

"It's okay to say the *D* word, man. I won't break down and cry." Jason hadn't in the past, and he wouldn't start now.

Wyatt shot him a withering look as they both sat at one of the tables. "They're total opposites, but for whatever reason, Erin and Jenna clicked. Jenna's her sounding board, her go-to for girl talk or whatever it is women do when they're drinking coffee and painting each other's fingernails."

There was something in the undercurrent of Wyatt's voice… Jason jumped on it, more than willing to shift the focus away from himself. "Jealous?" Wyatt and Erin had been best friends their whole lives, being born two weeks apart and running barefoot together around their family's land from the time they could walk.

"It's not that." Wyatt's eyes narrowed, and he seemed to be watching something Jason couldn't see. "You know how you know when someone isn't telling the truth? They're hiding something big?"

"Sure."

"Then you understand this thing with Jenna. The woman's got more secrets than the CIA."

Jason choked on a laugh. The humor felt good, easing some of the tension in his neck. "The geek is still strong in you. So is your suspicion of every female who crosses your path." Not that he could blame Wyatt. After what Kari Anders had done to him…

"I trust Erin."

Jason wasn't about to point out blood relatives didn't count. Wyatt had his own issues to deal with, just like Erin did.

Before he could change the subject, Wyatt pulled his phone from his pocket and read the screen. He shoved up from the table, his metal chair scraping against the tile floor. "I have to go."

Jason stood as well. "If this is about Erin, I'm going with you."

Wyatt hesitated, glancing from the lobby back to Jason. He tapped his finger on the side of his phone, then read the screen again as he headed for the hallway with Jason following. "They're putting her dad in a room for observation. You might want to lie low." At the elevator, Wyatt punched the button for the third floor. "I agree with you that we should keep an eye on her until we know what's going on, but you and I are both beat. I'll see if any of the guys want to make some money on their off time by coming here to keep an eye on things."

"I'll pay for it." This was his responsibility, his problem. The money wasn't coming out of Wyatt's pocket.

"You don't think you've done enough for her already?"

Not even close.

Jason stared at Wyatt until his former best

friend backed down with a wave of his hand. "Fine. As soon as backup gets here, we leave. I'm off tomorrow and we'll work out a game plan from there."

Jason nodded once. He liked plans. Thrived on them. They tipped the balance of control into his favor.

The doors slid open on the third floor and Wyatt stepped out in front of Jason, narrowly dodging a man in scrubs who was pushing a patient on a gurney. "Sorry." He muttered the apology then backed into the elevator, colliding with Jason.

The man on the gurney turned. "Well, Wyatt. You showed up after all." The voice was thinner than Jason remembered, but the harshness around the edges was impossible to forget.

Recognition planted Jason's feet to the floor and nearly dragged words he never said from his lips as the control he'd recovered wrenched from his grasp. Before he could disappear into the relative safety of the elevator, Kevin Taylor's eyes found his.

There was an instant of hesitation, a second of hope that maybe Erin's father wouldn't recognize him, but then those watery brown eyes turned to steel. His face reddened and he rocked up on his elbows, casting a look of disgust that ate through Jason like acid. "Barnes. What are you doing here?" Far from the weakened words aimed at Wyatt seconds earlier, these roared off the ceiling and echoed into the elevator, smacking Jason backward to the scrawny, unwanted kid who'd endured the wrath of his brand-new wife's very unhappy father. There was no battle plan, only desperate self-preservation.

"You bring him here?" Kevin turned his fury to Wyatt.

"Calm down, Mr. Taylor. You don't—"

"Don't tell me to calm down." Bracing himself on his elbows, Kevin Taylor cast a hard look over Wyatt's shoulder, his derisive gaze locked on Jason. "I told you years ago to stay away from my daughter. You're not worth the air you breathe. And you ain't taking her away from me. You hear me?" His voice cracked, and he swatted away the orderly who attempted to ease him back to the white pillow on the gurney. "Answer me, you—"

A nurse appeared and stepped between them to cut off whatever was coming next. She held out her hand, easing Wyatt and Jason into the elevator. "I think you should go."

Neither man fought. His expression grim,

Wyatt pressed the button for the lobby and kept his gaze straight ahead as the door slid shut.

Jason stared at the floor. He couldn't meet anyone's eyes. All it did was highlight the truth of what Kevin Taylor and probably half of Mountain Springs still thought of him. A nobody. A nothing. Worthless. A failure at protecting Erin once again.

Erin.

Jamming his finger against the button for the second floor, he turned to Wyatt. "Where is she? Right now? Because she wasn't with her father."

As the doors slipped open, Wyatt reached for his cell phone, his eyebrows creased. "I'll check the room. You check the stairs. She always takes the stairs." He pointed across the hallway at a heavy metal door.

Jason was shoving through the door before the elevator shut again, pounding down the stairs and fighting the urge to call her name. *Please, Lord, let her be in the room with her father. Please.* If she wasn't… If he'd let something happen to her while he was within shouting distance…

It would be just like when Fitz was killed. The guilt of two people's blood on his hands would kill him.

He pounded down the stairs and rounded

the landing, looking down toward the lower floor. His feet nearly slipped from under him and he grabbed the railing to keep himself upright.

Erin lay in a fetal position on the floor, trying to push herself upright. A red welt marred her cheek and her temple.

No.

He was at her side without remembering how he got down the stairs. Dropping to his knees, he eased her up to a sitting position so she was leaning against the wall, then ran his hands along her hair to feel for swelling.

She brushed his hands away. "I'm okay. I fell. Hit my cheek." Erin winced as she spoke, reinforcing her pain. "I don't think anything's broken. Just hurts a little."

"You fell?" Jason rocked back on his heels and looked up to the landing about ten feet above them. "Did you break anything?" He picked up her hands, checked her wrists and was reaching for her elbow when she pulled away again.

"Only a couple of steps. I was only a couple up when someone..." Erin stiffened and her eyes widened. "Someone pulled me down the stairs." The words choked her and she reached out, balling the front of Jason's sweater in her fists. "Somebody was here. Gray sweatshirt. Ski mask. Jeans. They grabbed me by the wrist and threw me into the wall and I missed the step and..." For the first time, fear whipped across her face.

Wrapping one hand around hers, Jason pulled his phone from his back pocket and texted Wyatt to call for backup. Heart pounding, Jason tucked his phone away and took Erin's other hand in his. Someone had attacked her when she was only feet away from him. Whoever was doing this was getting bolder. "They wanted it to look like you fell and were probably interrupted before..."

Untangling her fingers from his, Erin braced herself against the wall and stood, wincing as she did. She needed to see a doctor, get checked out, make sure she really hadn't broken anything.

Meanwhile, he had to find who'd done this to her.

He stood with her, but she edged around him. "I can't think this has anything to do with last night right now. I just... I can't. My dad. I have to get to him before he's in his room." She wrapped a hand around the railing and gingerly took the first step up.

Jason braced a hand on her back and bit his tongue to keep from arguing with her. He could tell her this was insane until his face turned blue, but she'd never back down. In the moment, she was more afraid of her father than of any conspiracy Jason could ever try to convince her existed.

Which meant he'd only have to fight harder to stay close and protect her from whoever had stepped out of his past to destroy the woman he'd once loved.

Every muscle in Erin's body protested as she slowed the Bronco to take the last curve near her house, finally able to bring her father home after two solid days in the hospital. Everything hurt, including her wrist, which bore bruises she absolutely refused to think about. They were a pulsing complement to the purple haze on her cheekbone. She'd allowed the doctor to run a few tests to reinforce what she already knew—that nothing was broken— and that had quieted both Wyatt and Jason. The pair had stayed in the waiting room until one of Wyatt's off-duty officer friends had shown up to stand outside the door.

Her brain still couldn't admit that everything was related. Angie Daniels's death had nothing to do with her. The snake had been a natural occurrence. Her father had fallen victim to bad food.

But the attack in the stairwell? Maybe Jason was right and she was someone's target.

Erin pressed her fingertips to the pulsing pain in her cheek. There was no way. Normal people from tiny towns didn't become the targets of killers. There had to be another explanation. A colossal coincidence. Anything but a series of targeted killings with her as the next target.

She needed rest, and then she'd be able to figure out an explanation. Her last shower was two days distant. The last time she'd eaten a real meal? No matter how hard she tried, she couldn't remember.

Erin silently thanked God for Jenna as she flipped the blinker to turn onto their long country dirt road. Nearly two days in the hospital with her dad while they treated him for food poisoning. Two days of him refusing to let her leave his side. Two days of him never noticing that her cheek bore a bruise or her movements were stiff and slow from her fall. He hadn't asked. She hadn't told.

Without Jenna, there wouldn't have been a change of clothes, a toothbrush or real food.

But man, she was dying for a real meal right now. Something substantial. A steak maybe. With a baked potato. And a salad. Maybe some apple pie. Anything but a sandwich. Jenna made amazing sandwiches, true, but a woman couldn't live on bread and fillings alone.

"Soon as we get home, you can help me settle in, get me some real food, then get on the lawn mower. Yard was bad enough before you let me get stuck in the hospital. I'm for dead certain it's harboring snakes by now," her dad said.

Erin shuddered. Snakes. Why'd he even have to go there? He knew how much she hated them. She hadn't told him about the one in the Bronco, but it was as though he knew exactly how to push the right button.

And as for the yard itself…

She needed sleep. Solid sleep. In her own bed. Chief Kelliher had someone covering her night shift for the next two nights so she could heal from her bruises and scrapes and care for her father, but afterward she'd be back on duty.

The thought of skipping a shower, a nap or anything else to mow the grass almost made her hang a U-turn and check herself into the hospital this time. Maybe she'd get some rest.

But when she turned into the driveway, her foot eased on the gas pedal. Her jaw slackened. She'd lost reality. There was no other explanation.

The yard was pristine. Mowed. Edged. Even the weeds along the side fence were trimmed. What in the world?

There was no one in the yard where the trees swayed in the light breeze. Who would…? Wait. The tailgate of a blue pickup peeked from the far side of the barn, almost out of sight from the driveway.

Jason.

Her skin heated with embarrassment and condemnation as she parked close to the house and killed the Bronco's engine. A quick glance at her father showed him surveying the yard. He'd missed the flash of blue behind the barn.

But… Jason? After the way she'd been rebuffing him and the way her father had acted at the hospital, he'd come to the house to do her a favor? A chore he hated above all others?

Jason loathed yard work. His parents had put him behind a push mower on over an acre of land from the time he had enough weight to get the thing moving. When he was emancipated, he moved out of their rental house and into the apartment above the garage at Wyatt's family home, where he did everything to help out except do yard work. She was certain he still lived in an apartment.

He'd joked more than once about how, when they bought a house, he'd sell plasma if he had to in order to pay someone else to handle the lawn. Erin had told him she'd mow every day if he'd clean the bathroom and cook, the two chores she hated the most. They'd sealed the deal with more than one kiss.

Erin almost smiled, but the pain of past dreams snuffed out the warm emotion quickly. Now she cooked, cleaned the bathroom, mowed the grass…

But not today, because of Jason.

No matter their past history, he didn't deserve the kind of treatment one of the nurses had told her about. Erin had tried to tell her father his outburst was out of line, but every time she'd mentioned Jason, the heart rate monitor had responded. Erin had given up.

This was why she'd never told him about her marriage. It would have killed him.

From the passenger seat, her father muttered a couple of oaths under his breath. She barely caught the words "Wyatt's good for one thing at least" and a couple more curses.

Best to let him believe it was her cousin who'd done the work, although the wonder of it still twisted in her head. "Dad, Wyatt's not even your nephew but he's always been good to—"

"Wyatt was spoiled rotten by your mama's brother and he still acts like the world owes him, way he wears that badge like it gives him some kind of edge over the rest of us. Wasn't for Wyatt, you never would have gotten tangled up with the Barnes kid in the first place. Least Wyatt knows how to respect his elders and take care of 'em when they're having trouble. The Barnes boy? Even his own mama was smart enough to get out before he could disappoint her."

So much venom. "That was a low blow."

Her father's head jerked back. He was probably about six seconds from losing his temper. "You gonna defend him? Really? He took my pride and joy, and he drove it down an embankment and totaled it. I worked on that car for a decade and he destroyed it. Besides, I don't see him around here doing nothing for either of us, even though he walked into my house after the wreck and tried to tell me how much he loved you. I saved you a whole lot of trouble by running that one off." He shoved open the door and eased to the ground. "Now come on. I'm starving." The Bronco rocked as he slammed the door.

Erin watched him shuffle away, anger and rejection at war in her gut. She kneaded the steering wheel with tight fingers, the urge to unleash her fury on her father a physical pressure in her chest. He really thought he'd done something good? Her father was the whole reason she'd broken Jason's heart and her own.

She sank into the seat. And she could never tell him. He'd been so agitated after seeing Jason at the hospital, the doctors had resorted to medication to bring his blood pressure back into line. She couldn't risk riling him into another stroke.

Having Jason around the house wasn't the best idea. With a longing look at the front door and a deep ache for her pillow, Erin finally turned toward the barn. She could walk away or she could go through the door and thank Jason for what he'd done. What he'd sacrificed.

For her.

But to do so would change everything.

SEVEN

Jason tightened the oil cap and rocked back on his heels, staring at the red riding mower he'd spent more than half of the previous day on. He hadn't voluntarily mowed grass in…

Well, ever.

Before his parents left, the yard was his job and he'd hated it. Hated the way his dad would lock him out of the house until the job was done. Or pack up his mom and leave. There had been more than a few nights he'd slept on the porch when they didn't come back.

He'd vowed never to push a mower again.

The army had different ideas, though. Jason smirked. He'd learned quick how to stay out of the kind of trouble that earned extra duty, or how to talk his way into any other job than walking behind a mower in the company area.

He'd sat in the seat of the riding mower

for a good five minutes yesterday, wondering what he was doing here, why he even cared if Kevin Taylor's grass was cut. He had no obligation to the man or to Erin during the time Wyatt had one of his buddies standing watch at the hospital.

But when he'd realized that nothing had changed in the Taylor household, Jason couldn't let Erin carry the burden, especially when she had to be in pain from the attack in the stairwell. She had enough on her plate, and Jason himself had dropped a whole bunch of rotten right into her lap. If he couldn't be at the hospital for fear of making things even worse with Erin, he could at least do this for her. He would help her from a distance, even if it was the one thing on earth he hated most.

He'd assumed the job would be torture, but after the first few minutes he'd eased into the job. With two officers watching Erin at the hospital, he'd been able to shift his focus. His thoughts had eased into a mindless back-and-forth rhythm, and he admitted a riding mower was a whole lot different from a push mower.

With his brain free, he'd run through every mission the team had been on during their last disastrous deployment… Cataloged who they'd taken out… Where the cells might be active now… Who might have the strongest motives for revenge…

And who could possibly have the access needed to find their wives and to wreak this kind of pain and havoc.

The list was long.

Every time his phone buzzed, he tensed, braced for the next blow. A few of the guys had used their leave to take their families to parts unknown. Others had armed themselves for defense.

Despite two days of quiet after Erin's attack, his gut said this wasn't over. The text on Angie's phone wasn't for fun. Someone had aimed an arrow straight at Erin, and the bold move at the hospital said they wouldn't leave it hanging there without letting it fly. She was still in some unseen enemy's crosshairs.

The back door to the barn creaked open, and Jason came to his feet, ready to fight anyone who thought they could sneak up on him. He might be armed with a socket wrench, but he knew how to use it.

The intruder he spotted might be more dangerous to his heart than his life.

Erin shut the door and stood hesitantly near the entrance, watching Jason with an expression he couldn't read. It could be fear… or uncertainty.

Definitely not the anger he'd expected. He tossed the wrench into the toolbox and wiped his hands on a rag he had found in the corner of a dusty workbench. "You're home early."

"Not early enough."

Clearly. She looked exhausted. Jason didn't doubt her father had run her ragged the past couple of days. "How's your dad?"

"Better. They treated him for botulism."

"Botulism's a strange one. Where would he get canned food that had gone bad?"

"I don't know. Considering we eat the same things, it's even weirder, but I'm too tired to figure it out now. My brain is mush." She shoved her hands through her hair, then pulled her ponytail tighter. "I just came out here because, well… I saw the yard." She walked closer and stopped on the other side of the mower, her gaze on the cracked vinyl seat. "And then I saw your truck." She caught his eye, then looked down again, a hefty dose of amusement sparkling in her expression. "You used a lawn mower. That's…big."

"Yeah, well, it started as me helping Wyatt with it. Then he went back to work and…" The smile caught Jason off guard. The warmth in her eyes was something he hadn't seen in years and had never expected to see again. This was one of the things he'd fallen in love with, the way everything about her changed when she laughed. Joy made her a thousand times more beautiful than she already was.

It eased under his skin with a fire he shouldn't feel about the woman who'd already made infinitely clear he was never allowed back into her life.

Their history wasn't important anyway, other than the fact that it was the very thing that had put Erin in jeopardy today. He had to remember that. "We need to talk about what happened at the hospital."

The welcoming smile she'd held only a few seconds earlier hardened into an unreadable expression. "Thanks for taking care of the yard, but I think it's best if you leave before Dad figures out you're here. I don't need to put him right back into the ER." She turned to walk away, her shoulders stiff and her back straight.

"I'm not leaving."

"Yes, you definitely are."

"I saw the footage from the security camera."

Erin's steps stuttered, and she stopped, though she didn't turn back to him. "What footage?"

"From when you were attacked in the stairwell." Wyatt had let him sit in on the viewing, and it had left Jason with a cold terror in the pit of his stomach. The proof was right there, irrefutable. He'd wanted to keep the worst of it from Erin if possible, but her stubborn refusal to let him help made full disclosure a necessity. "You were a definite target."

Her shoulders rose and fell as she breathed deeply. Then she slowly faced him. "Tell me. All of it."

Jason wanted to close the space between them and take her hand, touch her shoulder, something to reassure her, but he couldn't. That wasn't his place, which meant there was no way to soften the blow. He might as well be blunt. "Shortly after you and I walked into the ER, someone else came in. He wore a hoodie, kept his face away from the cameras, took a seat in the waiting room and didn't move until you and I went into the other room. He changed seats to watch us, then followed you when you headed upstairs. Never once did the camera get a face shot. And the baggy shirt, the baggy jeans, the slouch in the walk… Wyatt believes it was on purpose, all designed to keep us from guessing at height, weight, anything at all. Whether or not the intention was for your dad to get sick is up in the air, but from the second you walked into the hospital, you were on radar. And the only way to know where you were was to be following you. Whoever it is has been watching the house, Erin." She had to see that, to understand why he couldn't simply pull up stakes, go back to his apartment and let either one of them live under the illusion that she was safe in her own home.

She wasn't.

Although her face had grown increasingly pale as he'd told her the truth he'd hated to speak, Erin's expression hadn't changed. She took in the information and scanned the exposed rafters above Jason's head, seeming to process the facts from a distance. Finally, she swallowed so hard he could see it. "You can't sleep in your truck."

"It wouldn't be the first time." He'd caught rack time wherever he could overseas, not only in vehicles but under them as well when that was the only shade.

"Dad never comes out here. If you insist on doing this, you can stay in the loft upstairs. The water's still on. Just keep the light off in case he looks out the window."

The loft.

Jason could see that room as clearly as if he'd just walked out of it two seconds ago. Filled with light from windows on both ends of the barn, the arched ceiling was airy and the space was perfect for the easel she'd set by the west window to look away over rolling hills and mountain valleys. It had been her refuge, the place she'd run to paint her troubles away.

The place Jason had known the most peace. Where he'd spent hours sprawled on an old futon trying to study in high school. Too often, he'd set his books aside to watch her paint instead.

She was the reason for his D in chemistry.

He couldn't sleep up there. It held too many memories. "I'll be fine in the truck. Trust me."

She shrugged and turned to leave. "Suit yourself."

"You still painting?" Jason winced as soon as the words hit the air. He was delving into the personal too fast. She'd never stand for it.

Erin stopped so fast it was as though a chain had jerked her backward. Her head tilted toward the ceiling, where the room above their heads rested.

"I haven't been up there in years." Without turning back, she walked out the door and shut it behind her, severing the fragile connection between them.

Jason banged his palm on the hood of the

lawn mower and bit back words he shouldn't even think, let alone say. That was stupid. Incredibly, unbelievably stupid. Of all the topics of conversation in the world, why pick the one that circled straight back around to their past?

"Idiot." Swiping the rag from the seat, he bent, grabbed the toolbox at his feet and headed for the bench to store it where he'd found it. Best thing he could do was watch Erin from a distance and save both of them a hefty dose of grief.

A deep rumble worked its way into the room, like a low-flying plane or a distant boat motor.

The timbre of her father's snores from the den said he'd collapsed in his ever-faithful recliner to catch up on the sleep he hadn't gotten in the hospital.

With him resting, maybe Erin could get to sleep herself. She'd been lying on her bed for almost an hour, trying in vain to slip into sweet nothingness.

Seeing bloody gravel and blank eyes every time she closed her eyes.

Feeling the ache in her shoulder and neck every time she moved. Twice, she'd almost been asleep and jerked awake at the sensation of falling down the stairs again.

Sitting up, Erin stared at the window, where cloud-dimmed afternoon light leaked through the gauzy curtains. Watery sunlight fell across the windowsill and puddled on the bright yellow quilt.

Usually, she loved the soft glow of afternoon, but not today. Exhaustion had taken over, leaving her bone dead in a way she couldn't remember since those sleepless nights after the judge signed off on her divorce.

Piled on top of violent figures, snakes and murder, Jason's return kept her mind spinning. He resurrected memories she'd once dumped in a grave and covered.

Yeah. Sleep wasn't coming anytime soon. Leaning across the bed, Erin pulled back the curtains and stared at the upstairs window of the barn.

Behind the window lay the Erin she used to be, the one she'd shut the door on when her father's care became her penance, the one who'd vanished when Jason did, packed away in his rucksack with his dirty socks.

She leaned her forehead against the cool window. It was probably a giant dirt factory now, with dust bunnies running amok and cobwebs coating her last unfinished painting, an old farmhouse on Campground Road she'd daydreamed about owning. Jason had teased her about the old house and the work it would take to make it livable, but she'd never been able to let it go. There was something about the weathered old siding and the tin roof. They drew her in. The porch wrapped entirely around the house spoke of rocking chairs and lazy Sunday afternoons. When their marriage died, she'd been painting it in the glory of her imagination, the work moving slowly because she was either fighting with Jason and too tense to paint or was distracted by his presence.

In the end, she'd found herself staring at the image of a half-finished house as she slowly came to the realization it would never be what her dreams wanted it to be.

Nothing ever would.

She'd shut the door the first day she'd spoken to the divorce attorney and had never bothered to open it again.

Had tried not to think about it. Had succeeded for years.

Until today, when Jason had mentioned her painting.

So he still thought about the good times too. They had grown fewer and farther between with each passing month. Those were

the times she still vividly dreamed about…
then awoke disoriented and sad all over again.

Yeah, she didn't need those dreams anymore. They could stop anytime.

She let herself search the small wooded area on the far side of the field where he'd hidden his truck out of sight from the house but where he could see everything. He was too close, and at the same time, too far away.

Rapping her knuckle on the window ledge, Erin started to let the curtain drop into place, but something at the far side of the barn flashed in the dying afternoon light. She tilted her head and waited, angling until the light hit just right…

A dark figure slipped along the barn, keeping to the long, dim shadows of early evening.

Adrenaline hit Erin in the chest and she reached for her phone, Jason's warnings pinging an alarm. She'd dismissed them initially, but with the attack at the hospital seeming to be all about her and her mind too tired to think rationally, the idea that terrorists were stalking her wasn't so far-fetched.

Erin grabbed her phone and gripped it until her fingers turned white. Jason was only a few hundred feet away, but calling him felt like giving up somehow.

Pride wouldn't do her any good if she and her father were dead, though.

Tapping the screen, Erin scrolled through the numbers, her finger hovering over the one Jason had programmed in at the hospital and Erin had vowed she'd never use. The darkening landscape and the hulk of a person who'd disappeared from her view drove her thumb against the screen.

He answered on the first ring. "Are you okay?"

The sound of Jason's voice shouldn't make her feel better. It shouldn't instantly douse the fear flaming in her gut.

But it did.

Maybe she'd fallen asleep after all, because this was definitely a dream.

"Erin?" His voice pitched into concern. "Say something or I'm coming in no matter what your father might say or do."

Out of the question. "I'm okay. It's…" *Stupid.* She was tired, high-strung and emotional…or losing her mind. Nothing moved outside her window now. Maybe she'd imagined it. "It's nothing." Hunting season was in full swing. Could be somebody her dad had let use the land. Could be the power company trying to read the meter. She was overreacting, and calling Jason to rescue her was the proof.

She'd never felt so ridiculous in her whole life, not even the time she'd blended the Pledge of Allegiance with the Lord's Prayer on student leadership Sunday at church. "Never mind."

"We both know you wouldn't call me without a good reason."

He had her there. There would be no *just calling to hear your voice* between them ever again. "It's just… I thought I saw somebody outside."

"Where?"

"Coming up the side of the barn to my left. But it could have been—"

"It wasn't nothing." His voice was hard. Through the phone, she could hear the truck door open and his feet on the stairs. "Whatever you do, don't come out of the house. Someone's right beneath your window."

EIGHT

Jason shoved his phone into his back pocket, then eased along the edge of the wood line, quickly sighting the shadowed figure at the back of Erin's house. The man crouched low, wearing what appeared to be the same dark hoodie and ski mask from the hospital. From about three hundred yards away, there was no way to get an idea of build or age, but he was definitely up to no good.

Creeping along the fringes of the trees got Jason only a few feet closer to the house. The distance from his position to the intruder was wide open once he left cover, a good couple hundred yards. If the intruder opened fire, this wouldn't end well for anyone.

Reaching for his shoulder holster to make sure his Sig was in easy reach, Jason assessed the situation, trying to plot a route forward that wouldn't leave him wide open.

The way the house sat in the large clearing left him no good way in. There was only rough grass barely covering a former field, no cover. His still-healing leg would have to carry him faster than he thought it would. If his knee didn't hold…

There was no sense thinking about it. With one last deep prayer, Jason broke into the clearing at a dead run, his focus on the man kneeling at the back of Erin's house.

The figure didn't turn. Didn't break away from the house, didn't notice Jason's approach.

Twenty-five yards, fifty… His heart pounded with adrenaline and exertion. His mind raced through every plan to proceed. He should have called Wyatt for help. There hadn't been time. If the guy had a—

He pitched forward as his foot sank into a hole and jolted his momentum to a halt. He landed on his bad knee with a grunt.

The gray Carolina dirt morphed into desert sand. Gunfire echoed. Fitz screamed over and over in pain, in terror, in an agony Jason could never unhear.

Shoving onto his hands and knees, Jason focused on the dirt beneath him. Gray, not brown. A former field, not a desert. Erin's property.

Erin.

In as smooth a motion as he could muster

with pain ripping through him, Jason rocked back onto one heel and steadied himself with his good knee, then drew his weapon and took aim.

The man at the house had turned, and their gazes locked across the remaining distance. There was a hesitation, a quick darting of the head to the left, to the right. Then the intruder broke into a run, headed for the trees on the other side of the house.

Jason holstered his weapon as he pushed to his feet, but his knee gave way and dropped him again, the pain electric and shooting straight into his head. By the time his vision cleared, the sound of an engine on the road heading away from the house told him he was too late.

He dropped back to sit and pounded the ground with his fist, his hand sinking into the soft dirt at the edge of the old field. He turned his face to the clouds zipping across the sky. Stupid knee. Stupid war. Stupid... everything. He'd let their sole lead get away.

He'd probably blown out his knee doing it.

And Erin had probably witnessed his weakness from her window.

Hopefully, her father hadn't. He didn't need Kevin Taylor to know he was on the property. If the man landed in the hospital because of him, then every drop of the pitiful ounce of trust he'd managed to earn from Erin would evaporate and she'd be left without protection, a wide-open target.

His phone vibrated in his pocket and he pulled it free as he shoved to his feet, determined to walk off the pain. You okay?

I'm fine. Stay inside.

She wouldn't. He had no doubt.

By the time she crept out the back door and down the porch steps, Jason had decided the impact hadn't torn apart everything it had taken surgeons and physical therapists months to put back together. He fought a slight limp as he paced the perimeter of the house, avoiding the windows, alert to any change in Kevin's snoring from inside. He'd found a few boot prints in the soft mud at the corner of the house, yet no other clues presented themselves.

But those boot prints… They said more than he wanted to hear.

Erin slipped up next to Jason, who stared at the crawl-space access beneath the house. "You okay?"

Jason flicked her a quick glance, then turned his attention back to the wooden door with the small lock on it. The entry led to the underside of the house. Since the house was built into a hill, the door was about four feet tall at this point, but he'd guess the clearance dwindled to about a foot near the front porch. "Fine. He got away."

Resting a hand on his shoulder, Erin squeezed. "You're one man. You can't do it all." She pulled away and shoved her hands into her pockets. "I'm sorry I gave you a hard time earlier about staying. You were right."

In the past, he'd have gloated over such words. Now he wished he was wrong. He aimed a finger at the crawl-space door. "Whatever he was after, it was here, under the house. He didn't get to it, though. The lock's still in place." Wincing against the pain, Jason crouched and ran his fingers around the edges of the door. "Looks like he was trying to pop the hinges. Your dad probably put on the lock, but he should have turned the door so the hinges were on the inside. The only thing a lock does is keep honest people honest." He rocked back on his heels.

"There were some copper thefts a few years ago. Dad locked up the underside of the house because we have copper pipes."

"Makes sense." Jason looked up at her, try-ing to keep his voice level. "It bugs me how he didn't go for the doors or the windows for direct access. He was heading underground. There's not a way into the house from there."

"No, but there's something else." Erin sagged against the house, her shoulder resting on the white siding, her face cast in blue by the near darkness of evening. "The house is heated by a gas pack and has a gas water heater. The lines run under the house."

"Okay." Jason stood and brushed off his knees.

"So far, everything's been made to seem like an accident, a drug deal gone bad or a medical condition. If I really am a target and your bad guys want to keep it random, he could nick a gas line, let it leak into the house. Or…" She jerked as though something hit her in the head, then looked at him. "If it were me, I'd tamper with the furnace and let carbon monoxide do the rest."

The thought weakened Jason's knees. Bullets and bombs were visible things. Gas leaks and carbon monoxide? There was no fight there.

He leaned back against the house and crossed his arms, staring across the field to where his truck hid in the tree line. If he'd not been where he was this afternoon, watching… "I guess you answered my next question."

"What's the question?"

"Why he waited until you were home. The house has been empty for two days while your dad's been in the hospital. Ripe for planting a bomb. Filling the house with carbon monoxide while you're inside makes the most sense."

Jason glanced at Erin, but she was staring at something in the distance. She was doing that thing she did so well, where she distanced herself from the situation, shoved it outside of herself so she wouldn't have to deal with it. Normally, it worried him. Right now, keeping her emotions out of the equation might save her life.

The problem was, thanks to what he'd found at the side of the house, his emotions were squarely in play.

There weren't a lot of people Jason could trust right now. And as of a few minutes ago when he'd stumbled on those boot prints, the number had dropped even lower.

To two. Erin and Wyatt.

Praying he was making the right call, Jason opted for full disclosure. It was her life in jeopardy and she needed to know what he knew, even if it scared her. She'd take the threat more seriously, maybe let him stay close. "Somebody has inside access, and I don't know how deep their access goes. They now know I'm watching, because I tipped my hand today."

"You're hiding something, Jase." Erin stepped in front of Jason and held his gaze. "Your whole life, you've had a tell. Wyatt says it's how he always knew on the football field which way you were going to fake. Right now? You're telling hard."

"I have a tell?" Great. The last thing he needed was for the world to be able to read him. Check that. The last thing he needed was for Erin to still be able to read him. "What is it?"

Erin backed away, almost as though she thought she'd said too much. "I clue you in and you'll stop doing it. The rest of us lose the advantage. Now, tell me the truth. All of the truth."

Fine. Jason headed for the side of the house, motioning for her to follow. Beneath the kitchen window, he pointed at two impressions in the damp dirt. "Boot prints."

Erin knelt and studied them, probably noticing the tread and the size.

But she wouldn't see the thing Jason feared the most.

"Hiking boots?" She looked up over her shoulder at Jason. "Lots of people wear those."

"They're not hiking boots." Jason knelt beside her and aimed a finger at the tread, pointing to a double eagle logo in the heel. "It's worse. When we were overseas, companies would give us products to test, sunglasses, socks…boots. One company passed our team a specific design, one they wanted us to test. Even customized the tread so we'd be more likely to buy from them when it came time to make our next purchase."

"Jason. No." She understood what he didn't want to say.

Jason couldn't take his eyes off the logo, wished he could bury what it meant. He had no choice but to confirm her suspicion. "Whoever he is, he's one of us."

NINE

"Wyatt's still out there, isn't he?" Erin didn't know why she'd asked. Wyatt had followed her over the mountain into town, but he'd never step foot into Jenna Clark's paint-your-own-canvas shop. His presence was the reason she'd taken refuge here, because it was the one place where he'd keep his distance and right now she needed a break. She was trying to play this whole thing like she did accident scenes, holding the horror away from herself, standing outside.

It was getting harder as the threat grew closer.

Worse, the sight of multiple colors of paint had her fingers itching to pick up a brush, an urge she hadn't felt in years.

Jenna paused filling a tray with blue paint and leaned back to look out the window, her deep purple hair swinging. "He's eyeing the front of my store like he thinks I'm smuggling stolen art."

"Stop it." For whatever reason, her cousin and her best friend had never been civil to one another. "He's here because of me."

Capping the bottle of paint, Jenna set it into line with its cousins and planted her palms on the bar. "It's creepy the way he's following you, even though I know the reason."

"The reason makes it creepier."

"True." Jenna grabbed the paint tray and carried it to a family painting mountain scenes on their canvases. Tourists had packed the space, driven inside by the damp, cloudy day. The air was warm and carried the scent of the wood fireplace across the room. It was homey, comfortable.

Usually.

Almost an hour earlier, Erin had walked into Jenna's shop, hoping to grab a cup of coffee and some distraction before heading into work. Sleep had avoided her all night, and she was struggling to tamp her emotions out of the way. She wanted to talk about anything other than her unwelcome "bodyguards" or the way her own home was no longer safe.

A shudder shook her. She was here for a break from those thoughts. Typically, the bold yellow and orange walls made Erin's mood sunnier than a summer morning.

Today, the bright colors gave her a headache. She leaned heavily against the wooden bar. A holdover from the time when the building had housed Ridgerunners, a local watering hole, the polished bar top was cut crosswise from a single tree. Jenna hadn't had the heart to rip it out and now used it as the divider between the employee prep area and the customer tables.

Jenna rounded the counter. "Another guy's out there now, somebody I haven't seen before." One eyebrow arched. "The new guy's in uniform and…" She let out a low whistle. "Is that the ex?"

Erin couldn't see the window, but she had no doubt it was Jason. He could elicit a response quite easily in civilian clothes. She could imagine him in uniform.

Still, she didn't answer. Jenna and she had been friends for two years before she'd confessed her failed marriage and how no one in town knew about it. The story had intrigued Jenna, but she hadn't asked questions. Her silence was one of the reasons Erin loved her, because Jenna knew how to let secrets stay secret. It was the same reason she'd confided why she was being shadowed, because if she didn't talk to somebody, she was going to blow.

She'd also counted on her friend to find the humor in a horrible situation. Without it, Erin would go insane.

Propping her elbows on the counter, Jenna shot Erin a look sparking with mischief. "Girl, if a guy like that wanted to follow me around, I'd hand him a detailed itinerary and then I'd walk *real slow* so he could keep up." She wrinkled her nose and grinned.

The teasing worked, coaxing a smile from Erin, but it died quickly. "Yeah, well, there's more to life than appearance."

"What made you two split? It can't be he's mean and nasty, because no mean and nasty guy gives up vacay to make sure his ex doesn't die. So what? He's all gorgeous and no brains? He's a terrible kisser?"

"None of the above." Too late, Erin realized the implications of her answer. Her cheeks burned.

Jenna's eyes widened, and she straightened. "Wait. So he's nice enough to protect you, he's like all the best parts of a young and buff Clint Eastwood *and* he kissed you breathless? I don't see the problem."

"It didn't work out."

Forehead creased, Jenna studied Erin with

knowing green eyes. "This has something to do with your father."

No way was she acknowledging Jenna's speculation.

Turning toward the back of the room, Jenna untied the smock around her waist and tossed it to the counter. "Liza?" When her part-timer turned from helping a young girl choose a canvas to paint, Jenna aimed a finger at the back office. "Can you handle things if I take a break?" When Liza nodded, Jenna started walking. "Let's go, E."

There was no sense in arguing when Jenna got like this. Erin walked into the small square office packed with a bookcase and a huge desk. Painted plates hung over every inch of the walls, an even noisier riot of color than the main room.

Jenna shut the door and perched on the edge of her desk. "There's something I've needed to say to you for a long time, and the way you're acting, I think you might finally listen."

Erin's head jerked backward. She'd never seen her carefree friend so intense, had never heard her speak with so much authority. They were talking whether she wanted to or not.

"Your father made you divorce your husband."

"My father never knew."

"Wait." Jenna's gaze drifted as though she were putting together puzzle pieces in her mind. "When you said nobody knew you were married, you literally meant nobody?"

"Just Wyatt."

Jenna crossed her arms and stared at the space over Erin's head. "You got married without telling your dad?"

"That wasn't the plan."

"Keep talking."

She didn't want to. Rehashing events she'd long buried wasn't going to make anything better, but Jenna's expression brooked no argument. "Jason emancipated from his parents because they abandoned him when he was fifteen."

"Ouch."

"Yeah." Dropping onto the only chair, she plunged into the story she'd never told anyone before. "Wyatt and he were friends, so I was his friend by default, and then it was more than friends and then we graduated from high school and… And we'd always talked about getting married, so…"

"You eloped."

"We did." She sketched out the story with as few words as possible, from the wreck to her father's stroke and their decision to wait until he'd healed to confess the truth. "Weeks became months became two years. Then Jason joined the army without discussing it with me. Said he wanted to get away, to live together the way a husband and wife should. But Dad needed me and…" Erin shook her head and swallowed a sudden lump in her throat. It shouldn't hurt. The past was long dead. "Jason left, so I filed the papers."

"You do realize your father's stroke wasn't your fault."

"It was. And if he had another one because he found out what really—"

"Then it still wouldn't be your fault."

Erin shook her head, but Jenna didn't let her speak. She straightened and aimed a finger in the general direction of Erin's house. "Your father is a self-centered, selfish, horrible man who couldn't care less about you other than to have you tied to his side, controlling you until the day he dies." Jenna spit the words out like venom, the anger coating the air with an almost palpable heat.

Erin was on her feet, pulse pounding. "That's not true. He needs me."

"According to everything I hear around town, the man wore your mother down to a shell of who she was when she met him and he's doing the same thing to you."

"Jenna…" The word held every veiled threat she could muster. "Stop it."

"Tell me something." Jenna slid off the desk and closed the space between them. "When he blew a blood vessel in his head, was he upset because you were hurt or because his precious car was totaled?"

Erin opened her mouth, closed it, couldn't compute what Jenna was saying. He'd been concerned for her, angry for her. Right?

"I can guess how it all went down, sweets." Jenna shook her head, her eyes far away as though she was seeing something Erin couldn't. "He had a stroke and you had to take care of him, crutches and broken ribs and all, because it was all your fault. Didn't matter he'd never bothered to take care of himself. Didn't matter he'd never followed his doctor's orders. It was your fault, therefore you had to fix it. You had to give up everything so he wouldn't have to sacrifice anything."

Erin sank into the chair, her mouth open. "It's not like that." The protest was weak, almost drowned out by the pounding in her head.

"Oh, yes, it is." Jenna knelt in front of Erin and took her hands between her own. Her touch was warm, her grip firm, her eyes serious. "Nothing's changed. I've watched you knuckle under for years. Seen you sacrifice every dream you have. You want to join a bigger department? Can't. You want to paint again? Can't. You want to have a family of your own? Can't. He has you believing you owe him. Real fathers don't treat their daughters this way."

"You're wrong." Erin's voice was stronger as she stood. He was her father. He loved her. Jenna didn't understand. No one did. "Why would you say that?"

Jenna stood abruptly and looked at the office door.

Before Erin could process her actions, she turned and found herself face-to-face with Jason in the small space. Wyatt stood behind him.

The shock drove her two steps back, and her hip collided with the desk. The room was already impossibly tiny, but Jason seemed to fill every bit of it.

And she'd been right about the uniform. He filled it out as though it were cut just for him. He wore it with an air of authority and confidence that stole her breath.

But his expression stopped her cold. His blue eyes were intense, and the instant they found hers, there was no doubt.

More trouble was headed her way.

* * *

Everything Jason needed to say evaporated the instant he stood before Erin, lost in a haze of what used to be. Her eyes had run from the top of his head to his desert boots, and there'd been a flash of the old her, the one who'd lit his battered heart. It turned out she still had the power to warm the hidden crevices he'd buried over years of brutal deployments, and the emotion almost knocked him back into the hallway.

But as soon as her gaze caught his, the fire shifted to fear and jerked him into the present reality. He wasn't allowed to feel for her, not when it could cost them both everything. She was in danger…and the news Wyatt had delivered amped the need to throw all of his resources into keeping her safe.

He started to reach for her to ensure her focus but stopped. His heart had already set his feet on a path toward something that would end with him destroyed once again. She was his mission, nothing more.

Someone was dragging her in deeper and she deserved to know. He let his hands fall to his sides, his fists clenched. "We need to talk."

Her forehead wrinkled. Then her attention

fell to the rank on his chest. "Why are you in uniform?"

Not the question he'd expected. It derailed his planned speech. "I… They called the unit in for a video teleconference with all of the soldiers attached to us on our last deployment to brief everyone on the latest." The conference had yielded nothing new. No one else had been killed, but the quiet didn't ease the deep worry on the faces of the men in the room with him or on video from around the world. Dozens of men who had been boots on the ground with their unit or who had supported them with intel and supplies. Although only his direct platoon had been hit so far, no one was truly safe.

"They're still pursuing the terror-cell aspect." He'd called Major Jackson aside and told him about the boot prints at Erin's house, leaving it to the chain of command to decide how to proceed with the information. It could be a red herring…or it could be condemning evidence pointing toward one of their own as a traitor.

That was the least of his immediate worries. As Wyatt slipped past Jason into the crowded room, the motion edged him until he stood looking down at Erin, only a couple of inches separating them.

She watched him with haunted eyes. "They told you something at your meeting. Something to say what's happening to me is only going to get worse." Her teeth dug into her bottom lip, a gesture he recognized. The truth was sinking in and Erin was more afraid than she'd ever let on.

"It wasn't the meeting." He had to fight his own muscles to keep them from reaching for her. His jaw ached from the tension, and he shifted it back and forth before he could speak. "It's something Wyatt found."

Erin's attention shifted to her cousin, though she didn't back away from Jason. "Tell me." Anyone who didn't know her the way Jason did would think the bravado was real, but it was as fake as the counterfeit money his platoon had once found in a shipping container in Mosul. Her eyes, her stance, the tautness of her voice… Reality was setting in.

"After you got back from the hospital, I had a hunch. Botulism isn't something you see every day, and nothing in your house would indicate it could be a problem. So I…" Jason's expression grew almost sheepish before he reset his no-nonsense soldier face and continued. "I had Wyatt take the trash from your house in order—"

"You did what?" Erin's voice pitched to an impossible level.

"Wyatt." A woman Jason hadn't even noticed straightened from where she'd been standing in the corner farthest from the door. Her dark purple hair hung to her shoulders, and she eyed Wyatt with a wary gaze. This must be Jenna. "Who steals someone's trash?"

The tension between Jenna and Wyatt was almost physical. He didn't even acknowledge her, simply kept his attention focused on Erin. "Someone who doesn't want to see his cousin dead."

The words rocked Erin backward and she sank to the corner of the desk.

Jenna sat beside her, wrapping an arm around her shoulders. "You couldn't have said it with a little more tact?"

Wyatt ignored her. "I called in a favor from a buddy who's an independent analyst and sent him the packaging for the food your father ate before he landed in the hospital. I trust what he found."

This was the moment when Jason wished he could grab Erin and run out the door with her, take her somewhere none of this could touch her. Where he could protect her. Because the fact was, he couldn't. What Wyatt was about to say proved it.

The air was heavy with expectation, but Erin said nothing. She simply watched Wyatt. A slight tic in her jaw betrayed the truth behind her quiet demeanor.

"There was botulism in the cake-roll package. As for the drink can, there was a small needlelike hole at the top seam. He'd have missed it if he hadn't been looking for it. Big enough to let someone inject the can, small enough to prevent a leak unless someone was really trying to get something out of it. The inside of the aluminum tested positive also. No way the botulism occurred naturally, not in two separate packaged sources. Somebody put it there."

"Which means somebody was not only watching my house, they were actually *in* my house at some point." Erin's voice was calm, matter-of-fact. It was as though she'd detached from the information and was discussing a stranger.

Jason hated when she turned inside herself, when she pulled away and prepared to go to the mat all by herself.

She couldn't this time. This was more than working through the sights and sounds of a traumatic accident. This was her life.

Jason squeezed his eyes shut then opened them again, letting his gaze drift to the window into the shop, inspecting customers, searching for anyone who might be out of place.

Because someone had gotten close enough to know her habits, her routines, her weakness for Pepsi and snack cakes. Someone had set a trap designed specifically for her. They could be anywhere right now. The fire station. Her car.

They'd gotten close enough to spike her food, had managed to get into her house even though her father was always home. They could do it again.

He needed more eyes on her, but with the boot print at her house, Jason wasn't sure who he could trust. The men he'd gone into combat with, had suffered and grieved with… One of them could be a killer.

A very cunning killer.

The truth cut worse than any bullet.

Motion drew him back into the room. Erin stood, shrugging Jenna's arm from her shoulders. "I need a minute." Without making eye contact, she brushed past Jason and out the door, hanging a left away from the main storefront.

Jason turned to follow, but Jenna pressed a hand against his chest. "Let her go."

Jaw tight, he eyed the woman who'd stepped

between Erin and him. He didn't know her, and she didn't get to tell him what to do, not when it came to Erin. Gently, he pulled her hand away from his chest and stepped around her into the hall just as the exit door at the back of the building slipped shut.

Erin was leaning against the aged brick wall, staring at the back of the camping equipment store across the small alley. Her expression was blank, though she turned to shoot Jason the evil eye when he took up a position against the wall beside her.

He couldn't blame her. "You shouldn't be out here. Not by yourself."

She puffed her cheeks and exhaled, her breath visible in the damp, chilly air. "I needed a minute to myself. I doubt anyone is skulking around town this time of day."

Chances were high that whoever was targeting the spouses in his unit wasn't pulling back, even in downtown Mountain Springs in the middle of the day. The brazen attack on Erin at the hospital was a pretty good indicator.

She probably didn't need to hear that right now, though, not when she was trying to assimilate the fact that her father had fallen victim and the killer had been in her house. She'd figure it out soon enough.

"What now?" Her voice was quiet, resigned.

If he had his way, *what now* would include pulling her to his chest and letting her rest there in a place where she could safely fall apart instead of building taller walls around herself. Even when they were married, she'd only allowed herself that luxury a few times. Now? The chances were impossible. She'd just keep stuffing the fear until she blew.

He just hoped he'd be around to pick up the pieces when she did.

"What now?" Jason took the tactical approach to the question. It was the answer she was looking for anyway. "Wyatt and I have talked. He's on night duty right now. I'll take point on keeping an eye on you, and he'll cover for a few hours when he can so I can get some sleep." He shoved his hands in his pockets to keep from reaching out to her. "You won't be left unprotected."

"So this is my life now? Twenty-four hours a day, forever? Somebody watching me? You go back to work eventually, and Wyatt can't keep that kind of schedule up forever. Then what? You're asking me to live like I'm under house arrest. And, Jase, if we get a big fire call, do you plan to follow me into the building?" She tapped her head against the brick, eyes on the sky. "Something has to give. You can't ask me to live like this for the rest of my life."

"Not the rest of your life. Just until we catch whoever is doing this. That should be soon, because with the way he's willing to strike in the open during the day like he did at the hospital? He'll slip up soon."

"Assuming there's only one person. You said it could be a terror cell, and that implies an army of men who are ready to—"

"One thing at a time, kiddo." This time, he did reach for her, slipping his arm around her shoulders and pulling her to his side, then resting his cheek on her head. "Don't go borrowing trouble."

He expected her to pull away.

She didn't.

Instead she sighed and seemed to sink against him, apparently willing to let him carry her burden for a moment. "How did they find me? You and I aren't linked anymore. What made them come after me?"

Fighting to keep his shoulders from stiffening, Jason merely shrugged. He had his suspicions, and they revolved around several things he'd done over the years since he'd left. The last thing he wanted Erin to know was he'd held on to a slim tie to her. She'd misunderstand his motives, might even accuse him of trying to win her back, even though none of that was important right now.

When he'd joined the army and filled out his paperwork, he'd made Erin the beneficiary of his life insurance. At the time, it had been because he couldn't think of anyone else. But over the years, he'd left it, hoping that if something happened to him, it would give her a way to separate herself from her father should the need arise.

With rogue hackers busting into government databases and offering the information they stole to the highest bidder, anyone could have access to all sorts of personal information for every soldier in the army, including the names, addresses and Social Security numbers of their beneficiaries.

"You're quiet." She eased away from him and turned to face him. "What are you not saying?"

"Nothing." He had no proof, no good way to tell her what he'd done.

No good way to say that his plan to protect her might be the very thing that got her killed.

TEN

Erin stood in the doorway of the bay and stared at the fire trucks she wasn't allowed to touch.

On his way out the door, Chief Kelliher had aimed a finger straight at her. *I came in the other morning to trucks polished so shiny I could hardly look at them without going blind. Not tonight, Taylor. Get some rest.*

Clearly, he didn't understand the only way she could silence her brain was by making chrome shine. Her first night back at work and already—half an hour in—there was no doubt it was going to be a long one.

While she didn't want any calls indicating tragedy for someone else, if she had to stay here all night in the deep silence with her own thoughts, she'd lose it. They'd find her scrubbing the roof tomorrow morning with a toothbrush.

There had to be another way to find a distraction. She'd double-checked the doors and windows a dozen times, had thrown away her stash of junk food, and had made a gigantic pot of soup from veggies Wyatt had bought and never let out of his sight…

Because she had to guard her food now.

She'd hidden in Jenna's bathroom for fifteen minutes after talking to Jason, trying to pray down the fear. Letting herself lean into him had cracked something around her emotions, and they fought back hard. She'd never had a panic attack before, and she'd always wondered what would push her over the edge. Now she knew.

There was no way to deny it. Whoever wanted her dead knew everything about her, from where she worked to where she lived… to the junk food she preferred. Someone had built a twisted file filled with ways to end her life.

Her stomach twisted around the food she hadn't eaten today. How had she landed here? On some killer's hit list with her ex-husband and her cousin as protection?

Jason had left Jenna's to get some rest, leaving Wyatt to escort her to the fire station. Her cousin was on shift with the police department now, which meant somewhere, in the growing darkness where she couldn't see, Jason was watching. Erin kept her feet rooted to the floor to keep from peeking out the window.

What would her father do if he figured out Jason was still around?

Jenna's words rang in her head. They wouldn't stop dragging out images of her father, of how he talked to her, of how he never seemed to be there when she needed him. It was as though her world had been out of focus and Jenna had shoved eyeglasses on Erin's face, bringing a clarity she didn't want.

But Jenna had to be wrong. Parents loved their children. Her father had a gruff way of showing it. Besides, she had to honor him, to respect him. Erin had sat in church with her mother. She'd gone to Sunday school. She knew how the Bible worked. Children honored their parents. Period. Jenna was simply coloring Erin's life with her own past experiences, whatever they might be.

But she couldn't excuse the way her father had treated Jason at the hospital or spoken about him at the house.

If she knew Jason, he was sitting in his truck, freezing, with a pack of peanut butter crackers and a Mountain Dew as fuel.

He deserved better.

The thought of inviting him into the very

room where they'd spent hours talking and watching TV in the past made her heart pound a little harder. Though if she was being honest, it was already working its way into the danger zone.

All she was doing was feeding the guy dinner, giving him a thank-you for having her back, even for mowing her grass.

She'd keep it light. Even though a huge chunk of her wanted to spend hours asking him a million questions about how he'd spent the past eight years, Erin wouldn't do it. She couldn't fall into even a friendship with him again. When the culprit was caught and Jason was gone…

She wouldn't be free to go with him. She would *never* be free to go with him.

She pulled out her phone. Come inside for a minute. That ought to bring him in. If she'd told him she wanted to feed him, he'd have probably opted to stay in the truck.

When she opened the door, Jason stood on the other side wearing jeans and a black windbreaker, his hair slightly rumpled as though he'd awakened a few moments earlier. It was a familiar sight and brought back too many of the wrong kinds of memories about a man she was no longer married to.

He didn't notice her struggle with flashbacks. Instead he stepped inside, his eyebrows drawn together as he tried to see past her into the building. "Everything okay?"

"I made coffee and soup. Figured you'd want real food over the Mountain Dew and crackers you're hoarding in the truck."

Jason laughed, the sound genuine and covering a multitude of years. "You think you've got me pegged, huh?"

Without thinking, Erin reached across the space between them, pulling an empty wrapper from where it peeked out of his jacket pocket. "Yeah. I think some things never change." When he'd been on his own in high school, the man had practically lived on peanut butter crackers and peanuts. If Wyatt's mom hadn't fed him, he'd have probably wasted away into nothing. Every time Jason had picked her up in the old diesel Toyota pickup he'd driven back then, she'd spent half their ride to wherever they were going emptying the wrappers from the cup holders so she'd have a place to shove her own drink.

The memory brought a reluctant smile. Yeah. Some things never changed.

Erin started to turn and walk down the hallway, but his voice stopped her. "Everybody else is gone for the night?"

"Yes, so you need to help me eat this giant

pot of soup." The words cracked in her dry mouth. The longer she stood in front of him, the more she noticed his eyes picking up the dim light in the hall and reflecting like a beacon back to her. She turned to walk to the dayroom knowing he'd follow. All she needed was a second to find some balance before he figured out how much power the past held over her, power that weakened her joints, power she hadn't realized still existed until this moment.

When they walked into the office on the way to the dayroom, Jason chuckled behind her. "You guys are still using that ancient computer?"

She hardly noticed the bulky tower anymore, preferring to work on the faster laptop. "Chief Kelliher uses it. He says he's too old to learn a new operating system. It was hard enough to get him to transition to a flat-panel monitor." She smiled at the chief's stubborn streak as she passed into the dayroom, where there was a kitchenette, a couple of chairs and a TV. On the counter, a radio played a local country station, the song slow and plaintive.

Her amusement dimmed. The whole scene was too familiar, another mash-up of past and present to play with her heart and head. He'd hung out at the station every night she'd had duty when they were married. It was the one way they could find to spend quality chunks of time together. Because she was on duty, they'd only watched TV, but too many nights, she'd fallen asleep on the couch, her head on Jason's chest and his arm curved around her waist.

This was too familiar and easy and up-side-down and stressful all at the same time. It was like the day she'd sustained a concussion during a training exercise and the world had grown fuzzy and distant, as though reality had morphed into a dream.

Right here, in her own safe space, she couldn't figure out where to stand, what to do with her hands, what to say…

Apparently, it was a memory they both shared, because he hesitated in the doorway. "I can take something out to the car if you've got a thermos."

No. If he left, she'd devolve into a panicked, quaking mess. "Stay. Please." When his eyes widened, Erin didn't let it stop her. "The thing is…" She exhaled and sat on the edge of the recliner, wrapping her arms around her stomach. Now that she wasn't alone, the words wouldn't stay inside. She had to talk to somebody or the pain of what she'd witnessed would swallow her.

Somehow, Erin knew she could still trust Jason. Her gaze found his across the room. "The last time I was in this building alone, I let a woman die. I couldn't save her. I… I have all this training and…" The tangle of emotion at the base of her throat tightened and choked off what was left.

Crying wasn't in her playbook. Although pouring out her thoughts was necessary, showing this kind of emotion in front of Jason wasn't in the plan. Erin was mortified by the pressure crowding her eyes. "I wasn't enough." Twin tears traced her cheeks, blazing a trail she willed the rest not to follow.

There was complete silence in the room, no motion, no reaction. Erin stared at the gray tile floor at a point midway between where she sat and where Jason stood. It was a gulf between them, one that would always be there, one she shouldn't have tried to cross.

Their past made the present too complicated. Shutting her eyes, Erin swallowed and measured her breathing into a rhythm, although humiliation burned her neck and face. Jason had bigger issues to deal with. He was here to protect her out of a sense of duty, of obligation, whatever. But he was definitely not here because he cared about her.

The air shifted, and when she opened her

eyes, Jason was crouched in front of her, his blue eyes searching hers. "Hey." He wrapped warm fingers around hers. "You've had a rough couple of days. Nobody would blame you if you cracked, least of all me."

When he drew back and set his expression to neutral, disappointment Erin didn't want to acknowledge coursed through her. But there was a new knowing. She'd been able to block him out of her heart because he wasn't right in front of her in the fullness of all he was, in the flesh-and-blood man who'd once been her whole world, her future. Everything.

He was right to pull away. This was a dangerous game, and it was time for both teams to leave the field. She started to say something, but he winced and stood. Without a word, he walked to the kitchen with a slight limp, away from her.

Away from any chance they'd ever be more than what they were right now.

He was an idiot. What was he thinking, reaching out to comfort her? He didn't have the right, and besides… He'd say something stupid and make everything worse.

A twinge in his knee had been the excuse Jason had needed to back off and move around, get some blood flowing to his brain instead of straight to his foolish heart.

He grabbed the coffeepot, filled it with water and generally avoided Erin while she sat quietly across the room, probably afraid to say anything. What he needed to do was walk out the door, police the perimeter of the building, then pull surveillance from his truck. Erin could have her space and Jason could have his, because—

"What happened to you overseas?" The words were quiet, the echo of her exact same words from the first night he'd walked back into her life. Tonight, though, the question wasn't rhetorical or biting. There was an undercurrent of concern that had been missing the first time.

A concern that threatened to undo him. Shoving the carafe back into place, Jason stared at the top of the old four-burner stove. He never talked about Fitz's death. Ever. Not even with the men who'd experienced the awful day with him. "Why would you ask about my deployments?" He didn't mean for it to sound harsh, yet there it was, defensive and cold. Were the walls he'd placed around himself cracking enough for her to see through them?

When he turned to face her, she was watching him, and one shoulder eased up in a delicate shrug. "You limp. I wondered why, but it's probably not my business, so…"

Physical injuries. She'd noticed the limp, not the scars on his spirit. He took a deep breath through his nose and exhaled slowly through his mouth. He could talk about the physical. It was what ran beneath he couldn't bear to tell her, what had happened to those around him he hadn't been able to prevent.

Jason shoved a chair under the table as he walked past, then dropped onto the couch on the end farthest from her. He'd almost touched her earlier. Probably best to stay away from anything within arm's length.

In the small space, though, arm's length was pretty much all there was. If she leaned forward… "I blew out my knee running on loose sand. Tore my ACL." He could still feel the pop, the pain that had dropped him to the ground at the time his team had needed him most. She didn't need to know the sand was covered in blood and furrows where the enemy had dragged Fitz away.

"That's it? You were running in sand?"

He swallowed hard and stared at the ancient brown refrigerator tucked in the corner. Take-out menus littered the surface, most of them as old and faded as he felt. "Pretty straightforward."

For a second, he thought she was going to press, but then she changed tack. "And your shoulder?"

Unexplained anger welled in him. What was this? Why did she have to ask the questions he didn't want to answer? The ones he buried to keep them from rising and slaughtering him. Jason wanted to shut her out, tell her to stop being so intrusive.

But if he did, it would tell her he was hiding. He had to guard his secret at all costs. He couldn't let her know he wasn't the man she imagined he was.

Jason drummed his fingers on the arm of the couch and forced himself to meet her eyes so she wouldn't perceive any weakness. It took a second to trust his voice would be level and noncommittal. "An insurgent got a once-in-a-lifetime shot." At him, at his whole team… The shouts, the gunfire, Fitz's agonizing screams… If the room was quiet enough right now, he'd be able to hear them all over again, but the radio filled the silence.

Still, the memories chased him. He needed to stand, to pace, to get out of this shrinking room and into fresh mountain air not tainted with dust and gun smoke and death.

Before he could move, Erin leaned forward and rested a hand on his fingers, stilling them on the warm leather of the couch. She dipped her head to force him to meet her eyes. She hadn't gasped in horror, hadn't expressed shock or surprise or even pity.

There was only understanding.

No one had ever looked at him that way… except her.

The realization drew a hitch in his chest. In his entire life, he'd never let anyone see inside the way he'd once let her. Sure, his buddies were the closest thing he had to family, but even they only had shared experiences to bond them. They didn't know who he really was, at the deepest core of himself. They had no clue about the lost boy he'd once been and the found man he one day hoped to be.

Looking into Erin's eyes tore something inside him, ripping into the place where the real Jason resided, the one he'd shoved into hiding when he left for basic, the one who was safe with another person.

The one who had the ability to trust.

Erin's fingers tightened around his, and he responded reflexively. Her hand was strong, yet small and delicate in his. Until this moment, sitting beside her, speaking even the smallest sliver of the truth, Jason hadn't realized how on edge and unsafe he'd felt.

Her eyes scanned his, softening into an expression he recognized, one he'd seen so often when they were younger, one he'd responded to every time by drawing her close and pressing his lips to hers in a way every part of him ached to do again.

If he closed the small space between them and made the connection... If he kissed her... Then maybe the life in her would reignite the life that had once lived in him. He tugged on her hand lightly, an invitation to draw closer.

His ears rang in a way he couldn't explain, couldn't identify—

Erin stiffened and backed away. She jerked her hand from his and jumped to her feet as she turned toward the door.

The ringing... It wasn't in his ears. An alarm blared from somewhere deep in the building.

Erin jogged to the doorway of the office.

Jason followed, slow to react, his mind swimming in molasses, still lost in a moment he shouldn't have allowed to happen.

She stopped at the office. "Did you close the door when you came in? The one to the hallway?"

The tense professionalism in her tone

snapped Jason into the present. "No. I didn't have a reason to."

"I came in ahead of you, so I didn't close the door. I never close the door." Charging into the office with Jason close behind her, Erin grasped the doorknob. She tugged once, twice, then grabbed with both hands and pulled. "It won't open."

Jason tried to edge around her, but she held up a hand and backed away from the door, colliding with his chest.

She turned toward him, her face inches from his, her eyes wide. "Take a deep breath. Through your nose. Then please tell me I'm wrong."

Jason didn't hesitate. Obeying the command, he caught a sweet, tangy scent that triggered action. He flared his nostrils and jerked Erin backward into the dayroom, away from the rapidly increasing odor of gas flooding beneath the doorway.

ELEVEN

Jason grabbed Erin's hand and drew her with him into the dayroom, his mind working to put together an exit strategy. "Is there another way out?"

"Emergency exit off the kitchen."

Shoving her ahead of him, he let her lead the way to the door. She hit the bar full strength and the impact bounced her backward into Jason's chest.

The door alarm shrieked, but the door remained tightly sealed. "No way. Come on." Erin muttered words barely loud enough for Jason to hear, then heaved herself against the door again. "It's blocked."

Adrenaline shot lightning bolts across his skin. He eased Erin to the side and threw his full weight against the door. No movement. They were trapped.

He needed time to think, but the wail of the door alarm impeded rational thought. "Towels. Grab all of the dish towels and shove them under the door." It wouldn't help for long, but it should buy them a couple of minutes.

Unless someone lit a match. As strong as the stench was in the front office, the air in the hallway outside the door had to be saturated. If they were truly locked inside, there was a chance an explosion was imminent. Either that, or whoever had trapped them intended to leave them to die of suffocation.

Erin complied and returned quickly, her face pale and her expression tight. "Those towels aren't going to buy us much time. We either have to get the door open or we have to find another way out of here. I can smell gas in here now. It's getting thicker." She reached around him and turned off the stove, then the coffeepot.

Jason pulled his cell from his pocket. "We're going to need outside help."

"No." Pulling her own phone from the leg pocket of her uniform, she shut the device down and held it up, indicating Jason should do the same. "Cells, computers, anything electronic is a no-go. They can set off an explosion. Remote chance, but I'm not willing to take it until we have no other choice."

"Well, you'd better come up with something quick."

Erin ducked into the office, but was back as quickly as she'd left. She pulled her shirt away from her face. "Landline's dead. And I have a Wi-Fi signal, but no internet. Somebody's cut the lines." The tension in her voice betrayed her fear.

Jason was beginning to feel it too. The towels at the doorway weren't enough. The back of his throat burned. The shriek of the door alarm had taken a physical, pounding residence in his head and the gas multiplied it. If they didn't get out soon, his brain was going to mush into uselessness.

This was his fault. Instead of doing his job and keeping her safe, he'd stayed by her side, soaking in her presence, feeling like he'd come home. He'd failed her tonight because he'd been distracted by their very personal past instead of being focused on her very tenuous present. "This guy's slick. He's always searching for the next opportunity. We stopped him at your house, but this time I—"

"Don't start blaming yourself. It's not doing either of us any good. You couldn't have known he was going to manipulate the gas lines." Erin froze, her survey of the room coming to a halt as she turned to Jason, her guilt almost palpable in the small room. "If anything, I should have thought of it. This is my wheelhouse, and I suspected they'd do something like this when we were at the house. This is my fault. Not yours."

"This is nobody's fault. Nobody's except the person who's doing it. And now's not the time to be discussing this."

"You're right." She coughed, then cleared her throat. "It's getting thick in here. We can try the main door again."

"We don't know what's on the other side or if it's rigged to cause a spark when you open it. Everything so far has been made to look like an accident or like it was the victim's fault. Even Angie's hit-and-run was made to look like she was involved in a drug deal gone wrong. This guy comes at his target in a way we can't prove. A gas leak and a spark from a door? It's exactly his MO."

Erin was calm, her finger tapping her thigh as she surveyed the room, searching for anything to help them. She coughed again, glanced at the office and muttered under her breath. "Can't call out. And nothing in here is going to help. The only way out is through the windows, but they're reinforced."

The hope of escape propelled Jason across the room to check the windows above the couch. Sealed. Double paned. Probably bulletproof. It would take something heavy to break through and get them out. "Why so much security?"

"We have valuable equipment in here as well as some noteworthy items in the EMS supply room that an addict would love to rip off. We had to make it tough to break in."

Which meant it was tough to break out.

His ears rang from the gas and the alarm. His body tensed, waiting for an explosion to blow them clear out of this world and into the next. He could hardly focus on the task at hand, and the way Erin's voice sounded, she was flagging as fast as he was. "Hammer?" Maybe he could bust through the window.

"In the bay. All we have in here is basic kitchen stuff. And the chairs are wood. Not strong enough."

Jason studied the window and mimicked Erin, pulling his shirt over his mouth and nose. It probably didn't make a real difference, but the psychological effect gave him a boost. What he needed was something heavy, with a sharp angle on the corner. That kind of impact would breach the glass easier than a heavy blunt object. "Find me something with a corner, something that will make a small point of impact but has enough heft to put some force behind it."

"Tall order, MacGyver." Erin's brown eyes

were deeper than ever over the blue Mountain Springs Fire Department T-shirt she'd pulled over the lower half of her face.

Jason turned a slow circle, searching for the perfect tool. Most of the furniture was cheap wood. The TV was a flat screen, too light to be of any use. So was the computer monitor in the office.

But not the tower. He'd joked about the huge heavy ancient machine when they'd passed through the office earlier. Now it might save their lives.

He charged through the door without explaining, shut off the surge protector to keep the electricity from drawing a spark, ripped the cords from the back of the machine and headed back into the dayroom, where he stepped onto the couch and took aim at the window. "Back up." He didn't want to crack Erin in the head on top of everything else. "And pray."

She stood in the center of the room and nodded when she was ready.

This had better work because if it didn't, they were running out of options. Turning the tower so the bottom faced the window, he heaved the machine forward and smashed the corner into the glass.

A tiny indentation weakened in the center.

Three more blows to the same spot widened the hole until the entire CPU shoved through and fell to the ground outside with what, in any other circumstances, would have been a satisfying crash.

Erin appeared at his side with oven mitts from the kitchen, and they tore the glass from the window, gulping the untainted outside air.

And as his mind cleared, his thoughts raced through possibilities.

Grabbing Erin's elbow, he led her to the couch beneath the window, where they crouched nearly nose to nose. She seemed bewildered and he couldn't blame her.

"I can't shove you out the window."

Her eyebrow went up, but just as quickly, understanding tightened her features, deepening the creases in her forehead. "You're worried about a shooter."

"Not this guy's usual operating procedure, but he's coming at you hard and may not want to miss an opportunity. He's bound to know you were smart enough to get out or, if he's watching closely, he's figured out I'm here with you, even though I hid my truck out of sight."

She glanced at the window, then back at him. "I don't think we have a choice. He could light us up any second, and this place blowing like a bomb is a bigger concern to me than any bullet."

Erin was right. They had to give more weight to the known threat than to the unknown. And he had to get her out of here before the situation worsened. "I'll help you through the window. Zigzag for the trees to the right of the building. Get as far into cover as you can."

"What about you?" Her hand found his on the back of the couch. "I'm not leaving you."

"Right behind you. I promise." Slipping his hand from beneath hers, he let his fingers trail her arm to her neck, then pulled her forward and pressed a quick kiss to her forehead before breaking contact. There wasn't time for more, and even in his muddled, adrenaline-fueled state, he knew better than to give in to the impulse. "Let's go." He stood and helped her onto the back of the couch, where she straddled the window ledge, gave him one last long look and then disappeared, leaving him tensed for the sound of gunfire that would take her away from him forever.

Erin landed on the soft ground close to the building, her arm scraping the rough brick, her boots squishing into dirt still damp from recent rain. She crouched behind a bush, trying to shrink into the shadows, though anyone watching would have seen her descent from the high window. Her ears strained for the pop of gunfire.

Silence reigned. Even the wind through the trees was quiet.

Jason slipped to the ground beside her and hissed, "I told you to run."

A shove between her shoulder blades brought Erin to her feet and sent her sprinting for the small wooded area across the driveway.

The entire time, she tensed against the slam of a bullet into her back, but it never came.

They reached the cover of the trees and Erin dived in, taking shelter behind the sprawling trunk of a white oak. The minute they'd halted, she jerked her phone from her pocket and powered it on, the wait for the device to load an interminable decade of her life. Long enough to catch her breath.

Long enough to realize the warmth of Jason's lips still lingered on her forehead.

Taking cover behind the tree beside her, he focused on the station, likely watching for their attacker's next move. His mind was definitely not on her.

She waved her hand to get his attention. "We're not far enough away if the building goes." Even at this distance, the concussion of a massive explosion would scramble their internal organs and blast their brains against their skulls with a force guaranteed to destroy.

"If he was going to blow us out of here, he'd have done it already."

She tapped the screen of her phone, willing it to load quicker. "There's enough gas in there that it wouldn't take much. Even the heat pump kicking on could be all it takes."

"Can you open the garage doors remotely? Start venting the building?"

She shook her head. "Can't risk any metal on metal to put off a spark. We have to keep moving."

"My truck's on the other side of these woods. Let's get moving before whoever did this realizes we aren't inside. You can call for help from there."

"The faster the better. I'll feel a whole lot safer when we're about half a mile away."

Positioning himself between Erin and the station, Jason urged her through the trees, their feet crunching broken leaves and twigs with a racket that couldn't be silenced and seemed to echo for miles.

At the truck, they crouched low and Jason

opened the driver's-side door, urging her in. Erin didn't relax until he was inside behind her with the door shut and the engine running.

Her phone now powered on, she pressed the number for central dispatch. Erin didn't even let Kelly Wilson finish with her greeting before she started talking. "This is Erin Taylor at station seven. We have a major gas leak in the building and need all the help we can get. Dispatch police as well. We have reasons to believe this is deliberate. First responders need to come in with caution. Suspect may still be in the area."

"It was definitely deliberate." Jason shifted the truck into gear, then aimed a finger at the emergency door they'd tried to exit through earlier. A two-by-four was wedged tightly beneath the handle and the concrete sidewalk.

The sight drove a spike of fear through Erin, but she barely had time to process it as she answered Kelly's questions and made sure the other woman understood the assailant could still be in the vicinity.

The roar of the engine as Jason powered the truck away from the station nearly drowned out Kelly's responses, and Erin killed the call as soon as she knew backup was on the way.

Lord, protect us. And I know it's a building, but everything we need to keep this town safe is in it, so please... She let the prayer finish itself. The building was more of a home to her than the one she shared with her father. If it was lost, she had no doubt a part of her would be destroyed with it.

The interior of the vehicle was silent until Jason backed onto a dirt path into the woods near the main road, offering a small amount of cover.

"There's no question this was a targeted attack." Jason kneaded the steering wheel, his knuckles tight. "Whoever is after you is getting bolder."

Whoever is after you. The words washed a panic through Erin even more potent than the fear that had nearly swamped her at Jenna's. It paralyzed her and sent her thoughts into a whirlwind. She was a target.

Someone wanted her dead.

The carefully constructed walls around her emotions finally crumbled.

Her mouth went dry. It was one thing to hear Wyatt and Jason say it. It was another to be purposely trapped inside her safe space with death breathing fumes beneath the door.

Fear roared in her ears as she stared unseeing at the dark path before her.

"Hey." Warm fingers gripped her chin, turning her head. Jason laid his palms against her cheeks, his fingers in her hair, forcing her to look him straight in the eye. "I'm here. Focus on me. I've got you. You're safe."

No. She wasn't. Not at all.

His thumb slid along the soft skin over her cheekbone, sending a different kind of electricity along her skin. "You're the strongest person I know. You walk into burning buildings when other people are running out of them. You crawl into mangled vehicles when there's gas leaking across the pavement. You've rappelled cliffs to rescue stranded climbers. This?" Leaning closer, his forehead almost touching hers, he whispered, "This is nothing."

His blue eyes were deep, intense, the center of her whole world. When they dipped lower to her lips, her mind forgot to panic, forgot everything except Jason Barnes.

At the sound of approaching vehicles, Jason slid his cheek along hers and pulled her head against his shoulder, resting his chin against the side of her head for several long breaths before his body relaxed in some sort of resignation and he backed away, turning to stare out the windshield again.

Erin's eyes drifted closed and she slipped

away, pressing her back into the seat. If he was trying to make her forget her fear, he'd succeeded.

And if he was trying to crush her, he'd succeeded there too. Even if it had been the right thing to do, it stung.

"You okay?" He didn't move, simply stared out at the road in front of them.

"I'm fine." Her voice was tight, but he'd have to accept her answer.

"Erin, we have options. You don't have to stay out in the open like this. They've arranged for safe houses on post for the spouses who live off post and—"

"But I'm not a spouse, am I?" The words came out harder than she'd meant them to, eaten through by the terror of finding herself the prey of an unknown assailant, and wrapped around emotions Jason kept pulling out of her, emotions she didn't want to acknowledge. She had no rights to Jason and no privileges with the military. There was only a shared past that boomeranged closer with every second she spent in his presence.

The danger wasn't exactly what he thought it was.

Jason's grip on the steering wheel loosened, and his hands slid to his thighs. He sat for seconds that felt as though they stretched into hours before he spoke. "Our past is exactly the reason you shouldn't be in this mess to begin with." He lifted his chin and caught her watching him. "I should have protected you better."

Why had she mentioned their divorce? All it did was drive a deeper rift between them and now it opened him to some kind of guilt she couldn't possibly understand. "You didn't do this. You did your job as a soldier, and apparently you did it well. But this? This is the mind of some lunatic out for revenge, and you can't control him. All you can do is—"

"They found you because of me. Because I couldn't let go. I led them straight to—" He stopped, pressing his lips together so tightly his jaw muscles tensed.

In the distance, sirens wailed, drawing closer at a rapid pace. But the first responders were outside of the truck. What was inside was infinitely more important. "What happened, Jase?"

"Nothing." He turned away, staring out the side window toward the fire station, which was shielded from view by distance and tree cover.

The phone vibrated in Erin's hand, and she nearly dropped it. Not now. They were on the verge of something she wasn't sure she wanted to hear. But when the screen revealed Chief Kelliher's name, she couldn't refuse to answer.

With red, white and blue lights flashing shadows through the trees as help raced past their hiding place, she turned away and shifted her focus to the world outside of the truck, the one she had to find a way to wrestle back under control.

The one Jason Barnes was no longer a part of.

TWELVE

Erin swept aside the gauzy white curtains from the upstairs barn window and let the morning sunlight flood the room. Thick dust danced in the light, making the beams appear almost liquid as they fell to puddle on the floor.

Like everything else, it was a gorgeous illusion.

Sinking to the floor beneath the window, she leaned back against the wall with her legs bent in front of her and studied the room. Nothing much had changed. Yeah, it was dustier, but not as bad as she'd thought. It wouldn't take much to empty it.

Or to clean it.

This room, the one she hadn't given more than a passing thought to in years, had crept into her heart the past few days, begging for her to do something... To use it, or get rid of it.

She'd managed a couple hours of sleep in the predawn hours and had been awake at sunrise, restless, needing something to do. So she'd started changing the oil in the Bronco. But then Wyatt had taken over and she'd found herself here, searching for somewhere safe.

Someone had invaded her home. They'd invaded her fire station.

And now they'd ripped away her identity.

Once the station had been cleared and the crime scene techs had done their job, Chief Kelliher had taken Erin aside and told her, in no uncertain terms, she was on paid leave until the target was off of her back. *I can't put my other firefighters in danger or put this building at risk. I'm sorry, Taylor.*

Erin threw the oil-stained leather gloves she'd been wearing onto the floor beside her. She'd failed.

As a daughter, as Jason's wife and as a firefighter. The station had nearly blown to the moon while she was the one assigned to protect it during the dark hours.

She'd been distracted by Jason, had allowed someone to slip into the building, block the exits and damage the gas lines.

Now she was paying the price.

Even her own father didn't trust her to

drive him to Durham for his yearly physical at Duke. *Too much stuff happening around you, girl. Your uncle Joe's going to drive. Maybe I'll survive the trip.*

She should have taken Jason's suggestion to hide in a safe house. At least, no one else would be at risk.

But then she might truly lose herself, if she hadn't already. With everything else stripped away, this room was the one place the chaos hadn't invaded. Here, with a paintbrush in her hand, Erin had always become the purest form of who she was, as though she was somehow a little bit closer to God when she shared in creation with Him. Prayer had come easily here.

When she'd shut off this room, she hadn't just lost who she was with Jason… She'd lost who she was with God. Instead of deep, listening prayers, she'd started tossing up random requests during the day, half hoping they'd be caught by the One who was listening.

Not anymore. When everything else was gone, there would always be Jesus.

She dropped her chin to her chest and poured out every ache, every fear, every weakness. And she listened.

There were no magic answers, but peace

stole in as the light shifted across the floor. She reveled in it, silently praising the One who'd created her and who created alongside her until footsteps on the stairs had her swiping tears from her eyes.

Wyatt was likely checking on her, or searching for something to do since he'd probably already finished changing the oil in the Bronco. "Thanks for taking care of the truck for me. I could have done it myself."

"I'll pass the thanks along to Wyatt." The voice from the stairs was deeper than Wyatt's, heavy with fatigue but tinged with humor.

No. Erin might have peace about everything else, but she wasn't ready for Jason. She'd managed not to think about the two times they'd nearly kissed, shoving the disappointment she didn't want to acknowledge behind the more pressing need for survival, but he was still there, making inroads into her life.

He sat on the floor beside her with his feet planted in front of him and his elbows resting on his knees, his profile and two-day beard the picture of male perfection.

Erin turned her eyes to the back of her easel, which sat in the center of the room. Looking at him was out of the question until she adjusted to his presence. "What's got you out early this morning?" Dumb question. He was probably as keyed up as she was.

"I wanted to check on you after last night, make sure you were okay. And I wanted to run something by you. Part of my unit is getting together for dinner. We need to be together. We just need to…"

She hazarded a glance. "I understand." Grieving as a group was probably the safest thing they could do. There'd been many times she'd run to the fire station when she needed family, even if it was to avoid being alone.

"I know your dad's gone. If I go without you, there's no one to back me up. You'd be home alone, and I wanted…" He exhaled loudly, sending the dust in the air into a frenzied dance. "Do you want to come with me?"

It sounded like a date, but it definitely wasn't. It was protection detail. Nothing more. Her stomach sank. "Sure."

"Wyatt will be around today, so I'll come and get you around seven."

Well, okay then. Erin chanced a second, longer look. He'd had a shower. His hair was still slightly damp and towel-rumpled, a look she'd once known all too well.

Erin reached for the work gloves she'd laid beside her and asked, "Did you see Wyatt?"

"He was on the phone. Something about a crime scene on Overton Road."

A call about Overton Road meant her cousin would be busy. What had started as a simple burglary had exploded into more, though Wyatt hadn't filled her in on details.

She didn't plan to spend her cousin's absence by living out past moments with her ex-husband, even if the warmth of him beside her was undoing the knots she'd tied around her heart. This was exactly like high school, when her pulse jumped every time she heard his footsteps on the stairs.

When her muscles weakened at the sound of his voice.

Surely he remembered the times they'd spent here, just being together. Those moments chased through her dreams more nights than she wanted to admit. They'd had a very good thing once. Dreams… Laughter… Love…

Then it had vanished.

Erin squeezed her fist around the gloves, desperate to feel something. "What happened to us?" Her teeth dug into her tongue. Those words were not supposed to be out loud.

Maybe he hadn't heard her.

Oh, he had. Everything about him stilled before he spoke, his voice as soft as hers. "I guess…" He inhaled deeply and stared at the old red plaid couch, the lines around his mouth tight. "I guess when the foundation is weak it doesn't take much to knock the whole house down."

"You're right. We got married too young. Maybe if we'd waited…" The misery was as fresh as it had been the day he'd packed his bags and left without her. "Or I should have gone with you." She'd never said those words out loud, hadn't even dared to think it. She'd spent years blaming him for skipping out when he knew her father needed her, but maybe it had been the wrong call, choosing her father over her husband.

He chuckled, but the sound was bitter. "Or maybe I should have been less insecure."

Whoa. Of all the things she'd expected him to say, this wasn't one of them. "You? I can't remember you being insecure a moment in your life."

Stretching his legs in front of him, Jason dropped his hands to his thighs. "At first, I got why you couldn't tell your dad we were married. There was no doubt it could end badly, and I couldn't be responsible for something happening to him. But as the months passed…" He shrugged as though whatever came next wasn't important.

But it was. Because this was what they'd never had. The truth. An honest discussion. Everything had simply…ended.

Erin turned to him, legs crossed, her knee brushing his hip, hardly able to keep from grabbing his arm to force him to keep talking. "Don't shut down on me. I need to know. I need to be able to…" To find closure? To shut the door on them once and for all? Because even if she admitted she still loved this man beside her, the circumstances hadn't changed. Her father still hated Jason, and he needed her more than ever as the years piled on him.

Jason stared at the toes of his hiking boots. "Eventually it started to feel like you were no better than my parents."

The words hit Erin in the chest so hard she gasped. "What?" It was an exhalation, a barely there exclamation which held all of her shock.

His eyes had taken on a faraway look, as though he was talking without realizing she was beside him. "We were married. We were supposed to be family, but I was in the ridiculous position of living a double life. We had this amazing private world where we were everything to each other, but that world could never be in the open. I couldn't hold your hand in public in case someone told your father. I couldn't let anyone find out I'd married the most amazing woman in the world." His voice was husky, deep and fraught with an emotion Erin could almost feel. "It started to feel like it wasn't about your dad at all, but maybe you didn't want anybody to know. Maybe you were ashamed of me, and I wasn't good enough. Maybe I was the same kid who couldn't even get his parents to care, let alone the woman he loved."

Her heart tore. To think she'd made him feel that way, had wounded the man who'd never done anything other than love her. "Jase…" Erin breathed his name, held a hand out to him, then realized she still held oil-stained gloves. Wiping her hands on her jeans, she rested her fingers on his chin, turning his face toward her, and laid her palms against his cheeks, desperate to make him see. "Jase, no. I hated it. I never knew." Her thumb stroked the rough stubble at the corner of his lips. "I never knew you… I mean…" His eyes caught hers and all of the words died. His gaze held the same emotion it had held the first time he kissed her.

Before she could stop herself, she met him halfway, their lips brushing softly. She started to pull away but his hands slid up her arms, along her neck, into her hair, drawing

her closer. He deepened the kiss and she responded like he was fresh air after exiting a
smoke-filled house. Like he was everything
she remembered and so much more. He was
the man who'd always cared for her. The man
who'd made her believe she could be anything
she wanted to be.

He was her safe place.

He was lost. Gone. Finished.

All there was in the world was Erin. Time
folded onto itself as though they'd never been
apart. Nothing had changed. His heart shifted
into those places deep inside where he'd never
truly been able to shake her.

Her kiss still had the ability to turn his
world completely sideways, driving away
everything that had come before her or that
would come after her.

Almost.

The tiniest alarm fired off in the back of
his brain. He couldn't do this. He shouldn't
do this. She was still tied to her father.

And Jason had brought danger to her door-
step in a way he'd never imagined he could.

By sheer willpower, he broke the kiss and
slipped his hands from her hair, allowing
himself one last sweep of his thumb across
her lips as he watched her brown eyes and

prepared to break both of their hearts. Before she could react, he jumped to his feet and paced away from her, staring at the blank white wall, trying to get his pulse back to where it ought to be, trying to erase the heat of her lips from his.

Behind him, Erin's breathing sounded as ragged as his did. If he turned toward her before he fully took control of his emotions, he'd be on his knees beside her, kissing her again like no time had passed since the last time their lips had touched a lifetime ago.

What had he done?

More important, how did he undo it?

He swept his hand back through his hair and wished there was a way to reverse the past two minutes.

The problem was he didn't want to.

"Jason." Erin's voice behind him was low and determined. "I'm sorry."

He closed his eyes against the pain in her voice. "No. This was all me. I knew better than to come here. I could have trusted Wyatt to keep an eye on you, could have called you, but—" He waved a hand and sliced off the next part of his confession. *But I couldn't stay away from you.*

This room was a lost space out of time. It looked and smelled the same as it always had. Even her easel still sat in the center of the room, the painting of the run-down house she'd always had a soft spot for still resting there, exactly the way it had been the last time he saw it. This place was a museum of their past, and he'd marched right in knowing full well what it would do to both of them.

No, she shouldn't blame herself when he was the one who'd lit the match and played with fire.

"It's not that. I'm sorry you felt that way. I never knew." There was a rustle behind him. She'd stood, although he could tell from the sound she kept her distance. "I never considered how you felt. It was selfish of me. And if I could go back and do it over—"

"You'd still choose your father over me." He hadn't meant to say the words out loud, but there they were. The truth. The words that had cut him into pieces but he'd never spoken to anyone.

Erin gasped, but Jason kept talking, the dam breached. "It's not a choice you should have ever been forced into making. It's not a choice *any* daughter or wife should be forced into making."

Jason faced her, and when he did, he wished he hadn't. She looked stricken, as though he'd accused her of some horrible crime. In the grand scheme of things, maybe he had. Because he'd been laying all of the responsibility for the dissolution of their marriage at her feet, and for the first time, standing in front of her, he realized it was wrong. It took two people to build a marriage and two to destroy it.

He'd been wallowing in self-pity for so long, blaming his parents, Erin, her father for all of his troubles…

Yes, he was more of the problem than he'd wanted to admit. If he'd been a bigger man all those years ago, he would have insisted she tell her father. Would have stood by her and supported her no matter what the fallout. He'd known all along how Kevin Taylor held sway over his daughter, had talked to Wyatt more than once about it.

But he'd been selfish then, had never tried to rescue her for her own good. He'd merely worried about his own reputation, his own pain, growing increasingly resentful as the months passed.

Jason turned his face to the ceiling, where cobwebs clung to the exposed rafters. They were like the ones that had cluttered his thinking for years. It was as though a sudden wind blew them away and showed him his own self-centered soul.

He couldn't let her take the blame any longer. "Making it about you was wrong. I'm sorry." It almost hurt to say the words, they'd been buried under his own landfill of trash for so long. "I made it sound like everything was your fault."

"Maybe it was." She waved her hands in front of her as though she could clear the air between them. "It's ancient history. Over and done. There's no reason to discuss it. What happened..." She flicked her gaze to where they'd been sitting moments earlier, her expression heavy with the kind of sadness he'd sacrifice his right arm to take away. "It shouldn't have happened. I shouldn't have kissed you. I shouldn't have let myself get carried away by memories, because they aren't the present. And you're right. I'd have still chosen my father over you because you can take care of yourself. He can't. You have your health. I wrecked his. He's my responsibility. Mine alone. I forgot that when I married you."

The bald confession cut Jason so deep he winced. Sure, he'd said it first, but hearing it come from her mouth... It was the ultimate rejection.

And to hear her say, out loud, she still bore the guilt of her father's stroke...

Anger. Her pain fueled anger that threatened to force Jason into a showdown with Kevin Taylor. Because nobody... Nobody got to treat the woman he loved like she was worthless.

The realization stopped his thoughts cold and left him staring at Erin, his muscles going slack. He still loved her. This drive to protect her wasn't about guilt; it was about them. If a murderer took her away from him, it would wreck him. She was still the one who held his heart. Had always been the one to hold his heart.

Erin's head tilted to one side, and one eyebrow lifted. "Jason?"

He had no idea what to say. If he confessed, would she listen? After all, she'd kissed him, but then she'd taken it all back as quickly as she'd done it. She'd confessed her father came before him and would always come first. Whether or not she ever loved him again, he had to get her out of the house, away from a man who was slowly destroying the essence of who she was created to be.

Behind him, footsteps clomped on the stairs. Jason turned toward the sound, prepared to defend Erin, but it was Wyatt who came into the room, his cell phone still in his hand.

Jason's shoulders sank. There wouldn't be

any more discussion. It was for the best, because if he opened his mouth, all of the wrong things would probably slip out.

After one last unspoken question, Erin turned her back on Jason and focused on her cousin.

Wyatt stopped halfway across the huge room, his gaze bouncing from Jason to Erin. He had to sense the tension in the air. It was thick enough, alive enough, to start talking all by itself.

But when his eyes came back to Jason, it wasn't confusion or question sparking there.

It was pity, with a hardness around the edges that spoke of anger.

Jason's defenses immediately rose. Had Wyatt heard part of the conversation? Was he here to escort Jason out once and for all, to choose family over friendship, even if family's ideas were so twisted they'd dragged Erin into a stinking swamp to drown her in muck-covered guilt?

He started to take the offensive but bit the words back before they could leap off his tongue. His training had taught him not to move on assumptions. He'd wait, let Wyatt say his piece, gather his intel and mount a defense from there.

Wyatt turned his full attention to Jason.

"The phone call I got? It wasn't about the Overton Road incident."

Time froze. Just like the instant before Lisa Fitzgerald told him Crystal Palmer was dead, Jason could sense it coming. Another blow. More bad news.

Erin heard it too. She slid around the easel and moved to stand slightly behind Jason's right shoulder, the warmth of her presence infusing him with the strength to stand.

He swallowed hard. "Who is it?"

Wyatt exhaled loudly and stared at his phone. "Wilkes County fielded a call to an apartment complex near the base. Female in her midtwenties, went for a run, came home and suffered cardiac arrest. Her fiancé found her."

Fiancé.

The only engaged guy on the team was Rich.

Oh no. No. He was closer to Rich than to any of the other men. They'd trained together the longest, had split the cost of housing when they'd had to live off post, had been the token single guys all of the wives took in and fed… Until Rich met Amber Ransom and his whole world changed.

Amber couldn't be dead. They'd celebrated the engagement the night of Angie's murder and Crystal's death. Rich was so gone over Amber, so in love, so full of the kind of dreams Jason himself had once had… He couldn't imagine how Rich must feel.

But then Erin gasped behind Jason and he knew exactly how Rich's life was shattering.

He wavered and reached for the easel to regain his balance.

Erin's arm slipped around his waist and she moved in front of him, pulling his head close to hers, her cheek resting against his. Their argument was meaningless in the face of this new onslaught of pain. "It's okay. You've got this."

But he didn't. He didn't have any of it. And Erin could very soon pay the ultimate price.

THIRTEEN

Erin dropped the frozen chicken-and-veggie dinner onto the counter and stared at the package. She hadn't eaten since breakfast but, to be honest, she wasn't hungry and a frozen dinner held zero appeal. Pulling the freezer drawer open with her foot, she shoved the dinner back in, then leaned against the fridge. She crossed her arms and rubbed her biceps through her heavy Appalachian State sweatshirt. A relic from a happier time, it had always brought her comfort.

The house was too quiet, leaving too much room for thought. Erin was almost never home at night. Her hours at the fire station were designed to keep her close to her father during his waking hours. And she was definitely never home alone.

An empty house was either freeing or frightening. Wyatt was outside, watching the house, walking the perimeter. She'd needed a break from the constant supervision, but her cousin wouldn't go far.

On top of the refrigerator, the Ruger revolver Jason had given to her years ago rested. This afternoon, she'd slipped it from the glove compartment in the Bronco, cleaned it and loaded it. Even with her personal "bodyguards," something in her needed to be able to protect herself. The possibility of having to fire the thing at anything other than a target nearly buckled her knees, but the fact it was within reach gave her some measure of comfort. She could defend herself from an intruder if forced.

Too bad she couldn't defend herself from her own thoughts.

That kiss…

It had been the most natural thing in the world. The most right thing she'd done in years. There was no denying it now, not since she'd let herself go and allowed herself to feel.

Jason Barnes still had the ability to tug at her heart. The longer she was around him, the stronger the pull toward him came. The longing to fall back into what they used to be to one another was as overpowering as the fear of an unknown assailant.

And there was nothing to be done about

it, because everything that had driven them apart eight years ago still stood between them.

Wyatt and Erin had convinced him to go to Rich. He'd needed to be with his team, to grieve. He'd fought them every inch, until Wyatt insisted he would take the night off and wouldn't leave Erin unguarded.

After the things Jason and she said to each other, Erin was certain he wouldn't want her company anyway. In all the years they'd been together and apart, she'd never once considered how their secret had affected him, the weight he must have carried. How must he have felt every time she'd had to turn away from him in public?

Dear Lord...

She wanted to ask for forgiveness, to beg God to heal Jason's broken places, but the thought of his pain cut her heart in two and twisted the pieces in her chest. It was too much to know she'd caused him pain when she'd loved him so much. If she could go back and do it all again...

The truth cut even deeper than she'd imagined it could. As long as she was responsible for her father, nothing would be different.

If she'd truly loved Jason when they were married, wouldn't she have found a way to be with him no matter what?

This was why finding peace in the barn or acknowledging she still felt something for Jason didn't make anything better. Jason could only play protector and never be hers again, because while she was free in his arms, she wasn't free outside of them.

And he knew it.

While he might come back tonight to keep an eye on the house, he wouldn't contact her, and he definitely wouldn't take her to dinner with his team. In light of recent happenings, it was probably canceled anyway.

So she'd pulled on her most comfortable jeans and most comforting sweatshirt and re-signed herself to reruns of *The Andy Griffith Show*. A black-and-white trip to a simpler time might alleviate her stress enough to let her sleep.

Probably not. After Jason left, Wyatt had helped her rotate the tires on the Bronco. Then Erin had spent the afternoon in her room, praying for Jason and his team while Wyatt had given her space and stood watch somewhere outside the house.

Jason's team was on her mind constantly. She'd never been to combat, but she'd fought fires, worked accidents and performed res-cues with her fellow firefighters.

If someone was picking off the members of her squad or attacking their families…

Imagining their horror twisted her stomach. Jason's friends had returned from a combat tour that sounded as though it had been brutal. Now they faced this? How any of them stood under the pressure was hard to fathom.

Lord, help them.

It was the only prayer she had. There weren't enough words to cover a situation like this.

Her phone vibrated in her pocket and nearly shot her through the roof into the attic. It took a second to focus on the screen.

Jason.

Erin swallowed, tested her voice to make sure it wouldn't crack, then answered. "You doing okay?"

He didn't say anything for so long Erin glanced at the screen to make sure the call had connected. "Jase?"

"I'm fine." The tightness in his voice said he was lying, but she knew how he operated. He wouldn't talk about it until he was ready. "I'm about to pull into the driveway, and I didn't want to scare you."

"Pull into the driveway?" Erin jogged across the kitchen into the living room and peeked through the blinds. Sure enough, headlights swung against the trees as he turned off the road. "Why?"

"All of us are going to Lisa's? I told you I'd be here around seven. I mean, if you still want to go."

He still wanted to see her? After all that had happened this morning before he'd been slapped with more horrific news? "I... Sure. I have to change into something nicer than a sweatshirt."

"You'll be fine. I think since it's not as cold tonight, we'll be outside anyway."

"Y'all are still planning to get together, even with all that's happening?"

There it was again, a hesitation, as though he wanted to measure his words before he spoke them. His car eased to a stop behind her Bronco and the headlights were off before he said anything. "We all kind of want to be in one place. What's left of us, anyway." There it was. The nonverbal confession this was harder on him than he'd ever admit.

"I'll unlock the door and grab my shoes." She killed the call, twisted the dead bolt, then grabbed her running shoes from beside the door and sat on the couch to slip them on.

Jason opened the door, then hesitated on the threshold, one foot on the porch and the other on the hardwood in the entryway. He scanned the room before his eyes came to rest on her. "Is it okay to come in?"

With one shoe on and the other off, Erin sat back on the couch and stared at him. His wounds ran so deep, he still hesitated at the doorway of the house he hadn't set foot in since the week after their wedding. She'd been sitting on this very spot, her leg in a cast, trying to breathe through the pain of broken ribs, watching helplessly as her father cursed and railed and screamed at the boy he didn't know was his son-in-law.

Do you have any idea how much money I sank into the Camaro? How much time? What that car meant to me?

But no mention of his daughter. No concern for her pain. She'd never noticed it before. That day, he'd been furious with Jason for destroying the thing he loved.

And it wasn't her.

Real fathers don't treat their daughters this way. What if Jenna was right?

"Hey. You okay?" Jason's voice shook the thought away. Jenna was wrong. She had to be wrong. Because if she was right, then Erin had formed her entire life, had given up the man she loved most, for a lie.

"I'm okay." It was too much to think about with everything else swirling around her. She slipped on her other shoe and stood, stuffing her hands into the pockets of her sweatshirt. "You don't have to take me. If you want to go alone, I understand."

"No." Finally, Jason stepped into the house and shut the door behind him, his expression a faint echo of the boy who'd once had his whole world obliterated where he now stood. "It's easier to keep an eye on you if you're right beside me, and easier for us to protect each other when we're all in a group."

"Really." He didn't *want* her to tag along; he *needed* her to. Big difference. Big, life-altering difference. "I've got the Ruger, and Wyatt is—"

"No, it's not…" Jason stared at the coffee table, then at the blank television screen before he swung his gaze back to hers with the kind of certainty that wouldn't let her argue. "I already called Wyatt and told him to take off because, well… I need you there."

The muscles in her face slackened until she was pretty sure her mouth would hang open if she didn't think fast. He needed her. He wanted her.

Nothing computed. She was a job to him. A guilt trip he had to see through to its destination so he could move on with his life.

Right?

He took two more steps into the room and stopped a few feet away. His expression was open, earnest, more vulnerable than she'd ever seen. "We may not be what we once were, but I'm stationed here for the foreseeable future. Unless we go out of our way to avoid it, we're going to run into each other. And I'd rather not go out of my way to avoid you. Because, truth is, even though we can't go back to what we had, I'd like to think we can be something different. We started out as friends, then you were a constant in my life, and, Erin, I need you right now."

His confession nearly kicked through the last wall of her defenses. There was no telling him no. Since he'd walked into her fire station five nights ago, she'd been keenly aware of the hole he'd left when he walked out of her life eight years earlier. She'd managed to fill the space with so many things, but nothing had worked. Only Jason made her complete.

Erin nodded once, balling her fists inside her sweatshirt pockets, digging her fingernails into her palms to keep her emotions in line. "I'd like to be friends. I've missed you." It was one step farther than she'd wanted to go, but these were words she needed to say.

For a long time, they stared at each other, the space between them too close and too far away. She wasn't sure how to act. Hug him, or would that be too much? Wave him out the door ahead of her, or would that be too little?

Kiss him? Okay, so she really wanted to, and it was taking everything in her not to let her eyes go to his lips, because then he'd know.

The slightest smile tipped the corners of his mouth, one belying the seriousness of their situation. He held out his hand and she took it, slipping her fingers between his as though it was the most natural thing in the world. He squeezed her hand and opened the door. "Then let's go."

Erin sat in a weathered Adirondack chair and stared at the flames in the brick fire pit in Lisa Fitzgerald's backyard. The group around the fire had started with dinner in the house and now sat outside, silent except for the occasional story from the past that elicited a few chuckles or quiet sniffs calculated to cover tears, then dropped the group into silent memories again.

Even though she knew no one in this circle, to Erin the empty gaps around the small fire pit were obvious. This was a group in mourning, decimated by an anonymous killer.

There was really no other way this evening

could go. A group like this one fought black thoughts and emotions with stories of camaraderie and a dark humor calculated to help them survive experiences civilians would never understand.

The fire department was no different. It was the stories that kept loved ones alive, that made it seem they had only stepped away from the family for a moment and would be back as quickly as they'd vanished.

She studied the small group around the circle, as the fire cast flickering shadows on tired faces, and tried to remember names. Lisa Fitzgerald sat on the other side of Jason, leaning forward to listen to a story a red-haired guy with a beard was telling about Angie Daniels. Lisa had hosted the evening with grace and a delicate understanding of the balance between hope and despair, but her expression held a constant subdued grief. She clearly missed her husband.

Although the way she occasionally leaned over to touch Jason's shoulder or lay a hand on his arm made Erin wonder if the woman was ready to give love another chance.

Not that she wanted to think about Jason with another woman. It made the burger she'd nibbled earlier roll in her stomach.

The storyteller, Webster, was the single

guy in the bunch. To his right, a dark-haired man Jason had called Caesar fidgeted, alternately reaching for his wife's hand and staring into his empty cup.

Webster leaned forward, his hands clasped between his knees, eyes on the fire. "Sometimes, I think guys like me were pretty jealous of what Angie and Seth had. She had a way about her where she just kind of took care of everybody around her, always seemed to know what to say in her letters or to put into his care package when Seth needed it. Or when we did."

Erin forced a smile, but all of the memories she'd heard tonight lacked something. As the lone stranger around the fire, she wasn't able to picture Fitz or anyone else whose name had been mentioned over the course of the evening. And her only image of Angie Daniels was one that would haunt her forever.

Erin was the odd man out. These people had a history with Jason, had experienced things with him she could never share. It was disconcerting to picture the man she'd once planned on sharing a life with moving through life without her. Sitting here, listening to stories from their time apart, was like listening to tall tales about a movie character…or a total stranger.

Jason sat forward. "Remember the time Seth told her about the kids we saw in that village who didn't have shoes? Next thing we knew, she'd coordinated a shoe drive and we're all getting boxes and boxes of shoes."

Erin studied Jason's profile in the firelight. The shifting light and shadow seemed to highlight all of the ways this Jason was no longer a boy but a man. A man who had seen things most men never would, who'd braved the worst of humanity and survived. Even the way he'd kissed her had been different.

It was unnerving, almost as though he looked like someone she once knew.

"Know what?" Lisa wiped her eyes and laid her hand on Jason's forearm where it rested on his chair. "I had some pictures of you guys put into one of those photo books for my husband. He had pictures of those kids and the shoes."

"No way." Jason's eyes shone in the firelight. "I didn't know photo evidence existed. I always wished we'd had pictures. It was a bright spot in a terrible place."

Lisa held his gaze for a moment too long before she stood. "I'll get the book." She crooked a finger at Caesar's wife, Caroline. "Come with me, Caro, and we'll bring out some coffee."

As Caroline rose, Erin moved to follow. It would feel good to contribute. She'd sat like a lump most of the night. "I'll help."

Linking her arm with Caroline's, Lisa waved Erin away. "It's fine. Stay here." The two women turned and walked away.

Erin's eyes widened. She knew a brush-off when she saw one, even when it was couched in niceness.

No doubt about it, Lisa had eyes for Jason and she viewed Erin as competition.

She was still processing, wondering if Jason returned the feelings, when Caesar reached for his phone and stood. "I've got to take this." He disappeared around the corner of the house.

"His phone didn't ring." Webster turned to watch him leave. "I've been watching him. His anxiety's off the charts. He's probably got an energy shot hidden in his car and he's been waiting for Caroline to be distracted."

"Cut him some slack, Web. This thing is hard on all of us," Jason said.

"Yeah, but Caesar's been twitchy enough lately. Last thing he needs is to shoot his blood pressure to the moon or have a panic attack." He turned to Jason. "I used to be jealous of the married guys like Seth, but not now. You and I did it right, staying single.

Less to worry about now. Although, no offense, Erin, now's a crazy time to be bringing a girlfriend around." He shoved out of his chair. "I'm going to see if I can save Caesar from himself."

Erin's eyes slipped closed. *Single*. Jason had warned her he'd never told them he'd been married, but having it shoved in her face, especially with Lisa's behavior... Standing, she kept her gaze on Webster. "Good thing I'm not his girlfriend." The statement was catty, but she didn't care.

She walked away and headed for the back of the yard, away from a place where she'd never fit in.

Footsteps crunched through the leaves behind her, and Erin pretended interest in a dormant rosebush. Maybe he'd go away.

He didn't. Instead, Jason laid a hand on her shoulder, his touch warm through her sweatshirt. "Erin..."

Dipping her knee, she ducked from his grasp and stepped to the side. "It's no big deal." In a different universe, these people would have been her closest friends. She'd spent half the evening wondering what life would be like in this circle if she'd followed Jason on his military journey. Instead, she'd chosen a father who couldn't appreciate the sacrifices he knew she'd made, let alone the ones he knew nothing about.

She wasn't about to confess. "It's hard to look around and think about the missing links." Seth Daniels, Angie's husband, hadn't made the hour-long drive to the Fitzgerald home. Neither had Alex Richardson, who was with Amber's parents. Other couples were at Camp McGee or out of town, playing hide-and-seek with their unseen enemy.

"It probably seems like all these stories are out of place, but—"

"It's healing." She faced him, though she held some distance. "Lisa's fond of sharing stories with you." Erin winced. Why had she said that? Her mouth was completely off the chain tonight.

Jason didn't seem to think anything of it. Instead, he flicked a branch on the rosebush. "Lisa's a touchy-feely person. Always has been. Since Fitz was our team leader, she sees herself as the mother figure. There's nothing more to it."

Yeah, Jason was a man. Only a woman would see the competition in Lisa Fitzgerald's actions.

"Jealous?" He was looking sideways at her, one eyebrow arched, one corner of his mouth tipped in amusement.

She chuckled. "Not really, but if she touches you one more time, she might have to answer to me." *Whoa.* Where had that come from?

This time, Jason didn't miss her words. Everything about him changed, his expression expectant, warming her from the inside out.

She should put a stop to this, go home and call it a night before she said something really stupid. Something like *Maybe we can start over.*

That was something she definitely shouldn't say. The same obstacles stood between them as before, and there was no way around it. Still, the idea of belonging to Jason, of being a part of his life, felt natural, right.

And he knew it. Closing the space between them, he stood over her, looking down into her eyes, letting his finger trail her cheek. "Give me one good reason not to—" He stiffened and raised his head, something behind her capturing his attention.

Erin whipped around to follow his gaze. The upstairs windows in the back of the Fitzgerald house flickered with flame. A window shattered and smoke rolled out.

She was running before she even processed the action. "Call 911!" She shouted the command at Jason. She had to get into the house and find Lisa and Caroline. Nobody was in the backyard, and the women hadn't come out yet. Surely they knew the upstairs was burning.

Or had they already succumbed to the smoke?

A force jerked her backward as Jason grabbed the back of her sweatshirt and pulled her against his chest. "What are you doing?"

She jerked away. There wasn't time to argue. "I'm going in."

"No. I'll grab Caesar and Web—"

"Are you trained for this?"

"Do you have gear? A buddy to go in with you?"

There wasn't time for debate. "I'm going in. Call 911. And don't you dare follow me. I don't need another person to rescue." Without waiting for him to answer, she raced for the house and nearly collided with Webster as he ran around the corner. Erin sidestepped him, tugged her sweatshirt over her mouth and nose, and plunged through the back door.

Jason was right on her heels, shouting at Webster to call for help.

Smoke filled the darkened kitchen. The fire had already killed the electrical. Her head screamed this was foolish and she needed to wait for a truck to arrive with gear and backup, but her conscience knew she couldn't leave. With this much smoke, Lisa and Caroline would be dead within minutes, if the ceiling didn't collapse and kill them first.

Erin tried to process the layout, having walked through on the way outside when they'd arrived. There was an island in the middle, and an opening to the dining room straight across from the back door. Dropping to her knees, she found clearer air on the floor and crawled, the fire bringing an eerie twilight to the room.

There, to the left. Something on the floor.

Erin crept closer and her hands contacted something soft. A body.

She ran her hands along the neck, relief weakening her muscles when a thready beat throbbed against her fingers. "There's a pulse."

Jason ducked his head, drew a breath, then stood and hefted the body over his shoulder, leading the way to the backyard, where he laid the woman on the grass and Erin knelt beside her.

Caroline Augustus. And she wasn't breathing.

Erin drew Jason to his knees. "Needs CPR."

For a split second, she thought he was going to argue, but he leaned over Caroline instead.

Erin sprinted toward the house, desperate to find Lisa. Across the yard, Webster shouted into his phone as another figure disappeared into the kitchen.

Caesar probably thought Caroline was still inside. Now she had two people to pull out.

Gulping air, Erin dived through the back door. The heat had increased and the ceiling could go at any minute. She had to find Lisa fast, or they were both dead.

Erin dropped to the clearer air, but a sudden force smashed into the back of her head. She struggled against pain and the darkness, but the world closed in and everything went black.

FOURTEEN

Four counts in, Caroline sputtered and coughed, heaving in air.

Jason didn't know whether to cry or cheer. Brushing her hair from her face, he leaned close and whispered, "You're okay, Caro. You're okay." He rolled her to her side and held a steadying hand against her back as she gasped for air, his gaze searching the yard. Webster had disappeared around the front of the house, likely to gain entrance from the front.

But where was Caesar? And how long had Erin been inside searching for Lisa? Had either of them left the house yet?

Two shadows appeared in the open kitchen door, and hope surged in Jason, but the figures that emerged coughing and gasping were Caesar and Lisa.

Webster met them on the patio and lifted Lisa, carrying her away from the house as

Caesar's wild eyes met Jason's across the distance. "I can't find her. I can't find my wife!"

"I've got her!"

With a guttural cry that ripped Jason's soul, Caesar tore across the yard and dropped beside her as her eyes fluttered open.

"Caro." He whispered her name, then held her to his chest, rocking her against him. "This has to stop. It has to. I can't… I can't…"

Jason turned away to give them their privacy and to see if Erin had returned, his muscles taut and fighting to move. Still nothing. No motion at the door. The flames had burned through the roof and leaped for the sky. Through the downstairs windows, it was evident the fire was rapidly consuming the lower floor as well. To be moving so fast, it had to have been deliberately set. But by who? And when?

And where was Erin?

Erin had gone inside after Lisa… He had no idea how long ago, but it felt like an eternity.

There was a roar and a crash as the dining room window shattered and a shower of sparks dropped from the ceiling.

He was going in.

Jerking his sweatshirt over his head, Jason dragged it through the small fish pond near the fire pit, then tugged it back on and drove through the back door. Heat and smoke stung his eyes and seared his lungs, even through his damp sweatshirt. He couldn't see a thing but red through the smoke, which hung heavy in the kitchen, illuminated into a horrifying glow by the fire roaring around him with a sound like fighter jets buzzing the ground.

Searching for clear air, he dropped to his knees and the pain of his injury shot through him. Jason's breaths came faster, the visions in the kitchen melding with the horror of a firefight on a dusty Iraq road, of hooded men dragging Fitz away as Jason lay on the ground, his knee rendering him useless, his shoulder bleeding from an insurgent's shot, his team incapacitated around him.

Fitz screaming as they tortured him a few meters away…

His ears roared with more than the fire as panic threatened to overtake and paralyze him.

He had to stop this, had to find something inside himself to bolster him, to get him to Erin. To save them both.

How do I get through it? I pray. A lot.

It had been years since Erin said those words to him, so long they'd faded into obscurity until this moment. He could see her, sitting on the couch at the fire station after an accident on an icy mountain road had left no survivors. He'd marveled at her faith, envied it even.

There had been a time when he'd prayed too, before his marriage died. Before he listened to his comrade succumb to a torture he couldn't even imagine as the enemy tried to extract information from the Americans' leader. Before he'd grown convinced God wouldn't listen to the kid who couldn't do anything right.

But maybe He did. Because Jason had never dared to pray aloud for another chance with Erin, but his heart had cried out with hope even when Jason didn't realize it. And the way she'd looked at him tonight said this prayer might have an answer.

Jesus. Jason fought for air, his lungs burning from smoke and fire. *Help me find her. Please.*

There was no other way. Lisa's house was huge, a massive two-story with an open layout. Erin could be anywhere.

A crash and a new, louder roar from his left. More of the ceiling had fallen. He was running out of time. If he didn't find Erin soon…

No. He couldn't leave without her. If he retreated and she died…

He'd die along with her.

Lungs screaming for air, he crawled forward, scanning the floor around the island, but there was no Erin. To his right, the way was blocked by the burning beams from the fallen ceiling. *Please, God, don't let her be under there.* He couldn't let himself think such things. Not now.

He crept onward, fighting his watering eyes, trying to see in the strange, shifting red glow. *Help me find her. Please.* He pleaded with a God he knew had to hear.

His hands swept the floor as his eyes burned and watered and robbed him of sight. Heat seared his skin. He had to find her or get out. Find her or get out… Find her or…

He crawled headfirst into a door and backed away. There were no landmarks left. No way to know where he was, whether this was the garage door, a bathroom, a closet…

Rising to his knees, he turned the handle.

The door flew open with a momentum Jason couldn't stop and he tumbled backward, hitting the ground hard, a dead weight landing on his shoulder.

He rolled to the side and found himself looking into Erin's pale face. Her eyes fluttered open, drifted closed, then opened again.

"Lisa." She moaned once and tried to sit. "Have to find… Lisa."

He wanted to hug her, kiss her, reassure himself she was alive. But those things could come later. They had to get out. Fast. "She's safe, but we have to get out of here."

Adrenaline surging, he tried to rise to his feet but couldn't. He tried to orient himself as his vision darkened, either from lack of oxygen or the thickening smoke, he wasn't sure. He was at the pantry. He had to be. And next to the pantry…

Was a door leading to a side patio. He jerked the door open, then shoved a protesting Erin out ahead of him and barreled through behind her.

When she dropped to her back on the ground, he fell next to her, rolling on his side and inhaling clear air, stroking her cheek, brushing ash and soot from her skin. "You're okay."

She nodded once, then struggled to rise. "Lisa?"

Of course she'd be worried about the rescue. Before he could answer, someone pulled him away from Erin and shoved a mask over his nose and mouth. "Breathe." A face wavered in front of him, a paramedic probably. The cold air burned its way to his lungs, which gratefully accepted the oxygen pouring into him. His thoughts gradually cleared, though his throat ached and his eyes stung.

But he couldn't rest, not until he knew everyone had made it out safely.

Across the driveway, Lisa Fitzgerald sat wrapped in a white blanket on the back of an ambulance with a soot-covered Webster at her side. By an ambulance near the road, Caroline Augustus lifted a hand to her husband, who hovered over her, his face taut and gray.

And Erin... The paramedics had moved her several feet away and were tending to her as well. She appeared to be fine but Jason couldn't stop scanning the area, searching for more danger.

Because the fact was, Erin hadn't succumbed to the smoke or the heat in the house. There was no way she'd wandered into a pantry and shut the door behind her. Someone had put her there. Someone who had known she'd cast aside caution and go into the house after the other two women.

While all three women had been inside the house, Jason had no doubt the blaze had been set to target Erin specifically, and the pool of suspects had shrunk to the people he trusted most.

* * *

"Seriously, I'm fine." Erin held her arm out to the nurse who hovered by the side of her bed in the emergency room. "I don't need fluids. I don't need oxygen. I'm good." The argument might be more convincing if her throat wasn't scratchy and her head wasn't pounding so hard she had to narrow her eyes to keep the overhead lights from making everything worse. The spinning of the CT scan had been torture, and the wait for results was dragging on too long. This entire trip to the hospital was pointless. She was fine. Really.

If she kept acting as though everything was okay, eventually somebody would believe her.

She wanted out. To go home. To have a normal life, when terrorists didn't have her on some kill list.

Except the definition of *normal* was fluid at the moment.

The nurse left, promising the test results soon. After sinking into the pillows, Erin pinned a hard stare on Wyatt, who stood at the foot of the bed, looking a little pale around the edges. "You're sure Jason's okay?"

Wyatt nodded. "For the ninety-seventh time, he's three doors away acting as surly and stubborn as you are." When she started to speak, he held up his hand. "Lisa Fitzgerald is being treated for smoke inhalation. And Caroline Augustus was admitted for smoke inhalation. If you don't calm down and start promising some doctors you'll keep still and follow orders, you'll be the next to be hauled upstairs for an overnight stay. You took a hard hit to the back of the head. They won't play with that."

He didn't have to tell her she'd taken a beating. She couldn't remember anything from the time she went back through the kitchen door until she awoke staring into Jason's panic-filled eyes, but the back of her head throbbed in a way that left no doubt there had been a solid blow. "Did the roof cave in on me?"

Wyatt took a deep interest in the monitor beside the bed, which was reading Erin's vitals. Everything read normal.

Except his expression. He was hiding something.

"Wyatt…" He'd mentioned Lisa and Caroline, but what about the men? "Where are Webster? Caesar?"

"Neither needed treatment."

"So what are you hiding? You have a terrible poker face, almost as bad as Jason's."

Wyatt exhaled, but it sounded like a cross between a cough and a chuckle. He stepped away from the curtained doorway and lowered his voice. "Caroline Augustus took a hit to the back of the head, just like you did."

"How?" She'd found Caroline in the middle of the kitchen floor with no debris around her. It didn't make sense.

"The other guy? Webster? He claims he found Lisa Fitzgerald incapacitated in a downstairs bathroom."

Fear drove her pulse faster. Erin sat up and reached for Wyatt. "What happened to me? I remember going back into the house, but after—"

"I found you in the pantry." Jason's voice from the doorway drove the beeping of the heart monitor faster. He seemed to fill the space between the curtain and the wall, his face and clothes smudged with smoke, his hair wild and his focus on her. "Someone targeted you tonight. Someone who's…" His face grim, his eyes haunted, Jason pressed his lips together and refused to say more.

It should have shocked her. Maybe should have scared her, but a numbness crept through Erin that defied logic. With hit after hit coming, she'd half expected it, had essentially known from the moment she saw the smoke this was a deliberate attack. She couldn't think about being trapped in a pantry now, couldn't take the time to wonder how Jason had found her. She could only thank God he had, and she could only pray about what happened next. Going into hiding wasn't an option, not with her father in the mix.

Wyatt stood silently, his gaze going back and forth between Jason and Erin as though he were waiting for something. It was the analytical expression he got when he was puzzling through a case, not that Mountain Springs had many high crimes to worry about. But Erin knew the look, even if she couldn't puzzle through what he was thinking. After a long moment, he seemed to come to a decision. Pressing a kiss to Erin's forehead, he squeezed her hand and headed for the door, where he paused and said something under his breath to Jason before he disappeared into the hallway.

Jason didn't move as Wyatt passed, although the set of his jaw tightened and his gaze locked on Erin.

She felt exposed, as though he could see her fears, her frustration…her softening toward him. That was the one thing he could never know, because it would give him hope. It was a hope she couldn't act on, not as long as her father needed her.

She should end this right now, tell him to

leave and spare them both the fast-approaching heartache.

But when he sat in the small chair beside her and took her hand, the thought flew away, and only the here and now mattered. Here they were the only two in the world. Battered, singed, bruised...but alive.

Even if his eyes were haunted by something she couldn't understand. A smudge of ash along his cheekbone made the blue in his eyes deeper, darker. Erin ached to swipe it away with her thumb, but she had no right... even if he was sitting here with his fingers warm around hers. "What's wrong?"

"It's been a rough night."

"It has. But that's not it." No, this wasn't exhaustion or fear or even worry. It was something else. An anger and a pain hinting at deeper things, maybe even deeper than their past together. "What happened that I don't know about?"

Jason's forehead creased, and his thumb turned lazy circles on her wrist, an action he probably didn't even realize he was doing, even though it was quivering Erin's insides into mush for reasons entirely incongruous to the conversation. Eventually, he sniffed and stared at something on the wall behind her. "I don't think the person doing this is a terrorist."

All of the butterflies in Erin's stomach died. This wasn't about her. This was bigger and potentially so much more dangerous. "What?"

"That footprint at your house. I can't stop thinking about it. I was hoping I was wrong, but tonight…"

Erin shuddered. He didn't have to say it. "Webster, Caesar, you… Every man present was in Lisa's house."

"And nobody saw a stranger in the fire."

"Jason…" She exhaled his name and caught some of his grief. The men he trusted the most—his family—may have turned on him. "You've been through so much together."

"You have no idea." He was far away, as though whatever had wounded him overseas lay just on the other side of a veil Erin couldn't see through.

"Tell me what happened. What really happened." Maybe if he talked about it, he'd remember something. Or if nothing else, the haunted air below the surface would dim.

Jason started to speak, then dropped his gaze to their fingers, laced together on the white blanket that did nothing to stop a chill that had started in his heart and transferred to hers. Finally, he sniffed and started talking, though he never looked at her.

"We were on a mission outside the wire and had been for a few days, hunting a target who kept slipping by us." His fingers tightened around hers. "Honestly, we should have come in and taken a break but Fitz was determined not to fail and we were right there with him. Catching this guy, it was a personal challenge or something." His Adam's apple bobbed as his shoulders grew tight. "We hit an IED. Rich and I got out of the vehicle on one side, Fitz and Caesar on the other. The rest of the guys were behind us. We were ambushed. Found ourselves in a firefight. They were on all sides. I got hit in the arm, nicked, not bad enough to hold me down. But Fitz…" His eyes grew darker, his expression twisted as though he was in pain.

"You don't have to—"

"Fitz got separated from us somehow. I don't know how. It never should have…" It was as though he didn't hear her, didn't even realize she was there, even though he was squeezing her hand hard enough to cause pain. "They grabbed him. Started dragging him away. They pinned us down, hit all of us and…"

Tears coursed down Erin's cheeks, the images in her mind horrible and grief-filled, likely nothing compared to what Jason could see and hear in his memory.

"All of us were wounded. Medics stayed back with the worst, and the rest of us regrouped, went after him. They were torturing him already, in the back of one of our own trucks. He was screaming…"

Wrapping her other hand around his, Erin held on tight. He had to know he wasn't alone. She wouldn't let him go. From the way he told the story, this was the first time he'd ever spoken about it aloud, and she didn't want to violate or cheapen the trust he was placing in her.

For the first time, he was giving her all of himself.

"We ran for him, fighting back, but they detonated an IED in the middle of us. I took shrapnel to the shoulder, blew out my knee. It hit while I was running. Couldn't move, couldn't hear, couldn't do anything. And then there was silence. They tossed Fitz's body out of the truck, and it was… All I remember is blood. Mine. His. All of us." Jason dug his teeth into his lower lip and seemed to realize he had an audience. Gently, he extracted his hand from hers and sat back in the chair, staring at the wall. There was a long stretch of silence before he sat straighter and his expression cleared. "Lisa lost her husband. The rest of us were injured, some bad enough to medically retire. And the army sent the rest of us here to lick our wounds and to train other soldiers, because a calculated attack of such magnitude? That many men coming at us? Torturing Fitz right there? It was a targeted thing. One nobody on my team was ready for."

He stood and paced the small room, his back to her as he stared at the whiteboard on the wall. "And now one of those men? One of my brothers?" When he turned to face her, the grief on his face nearly crushed her. "One of them is a killer."

FIFTEEN

Erin leaned her head back against the seat in Jason's pickup and closed her eyes. Her throat ached, her lungs burned and her eyes itched. It was past noon on a day that had started years earlier. She opened one eye to peek at Jason, who'd overridden Wyatt on driving her home from the hospital. According to him, Wyatt needed more rest than any of them, and he'd better get it before he had to go back on duty later in the evening. "When was the last time you slept?"

"I sleep." Jason didn't take his eyes off the road. As the threat wore on without an end in sight, he'd grown increasingly quiet, his typical sense of humor waning. He glanced at her, then turned his attention back to the road.

"You sent Wyatt home to sleep. Maybe you should take some of your own advice."

"There's more going on with Wyatt right now than you know."

"Overton Road?" Whatever was going on, Wyatt had spent more and more time out there at the edge of the county line, where there was nothing but fields and a couple of old barns. "How bad is it?"

"Apparently, it's bad." His face shadowed, and a deep V furrowed between his eyes. "He hasn't filled me in on it, but he did say it's something he never thought we'd have to deal with here."

If Wyatt could say more, he would have already told her. His silence was more frightening than any tale he could spin. They'd had drug dealers and meth labs before, so whatever was going on, it had to be worse.

At the moment, Erin didn't even want to consider what could be worse. She'd heard rumors of human traffickers trying to get a toehold in the region, had been trained about warning signs. The thought of it turned her stomach. And if that was what Wyatt was dealing with, then he didn't need her on his plate too.

Both men needed her off their minds. They had lives. They were human. They needed rest and downtime or they'd both implode. It would be her fault when that happened. "Maybe it's time for me to move into a safe house, let somebody else do the watching. This has got to be hard for you and—"

"And I'm happy to be there." Jason kneaded the steering wheel with both hands, his knuckles white from his tight grip. "I know I pushed the safe-house thing earlier, but I'm not so sure it's the right call now. It isolates everybody in one place. Stop worrying. Neither Wyatt nor I have any problem with keeping an eye on you."

"It's not fair."

"A lot in life isn't fair." Flicking the blinker to turn onto the dirt road winding back to her house, Jason said, "Have you heard from your dad?"

"I tried to call him a few times, let him know I was in the hospital. Left a few messages, but he was scheduled for two days of appointments in Durham. He could still be at Duke with his phone off. Or he's not getting the messages. He has trouble with—"

"Stop making excuses for him, Erin." Jason jammed on the brakes and shifted the truck into Park at the edge of the driveway, an uncharacteristic anger darkening his features as he turned toward her. "You've been doing it for too long."

Erin drew her head back, the motion bringing a throbbing pain to the spot where someone had hit her. "What?"

"You want to know what's hard for me? Hard for Wyatt?" Jason jammed his hand into his hair and ran his fingers through it, standing it on end before he scrubbed it back into place. "It's not keeping you safe from a murderer. It's watching you kill yourself. Slowly."

Wait. Whoa. This was as left field as it got. "Nobody's suicidal here." Jason needed sleep. He was talking out of his head. "Maybe you need to—"

"Nobody said anything about suicide. You know, I always knew it was bad, but either my memory dulled it or everything has gotten worse."

"What's gotten worse?"

"Your father. He's destroying you from the inside out."

Seriously? With everything else going on, he was going to question her loyalty to her father? Had he and Jenna had a conversation about her? Because there was no other reason everyone would suddenly be coming at her this way. She was the daughter of an ailing father. He needed her.

And Jason Barnes was the absolute last person who needed to come at her about this. He knew better than anyone why things couldn't change. The man who'd abandoned her had no right to burst back into her life and question her now.

"All I know is this." Jason aimed a finger out the front window of the car. "He's home from Duke. He's been home since about nine last night. Joe heard what happened from Chief Kelliher and told your father, but he insisted on coming home instead of going to the hospital to be with you, with his daughter. Who nearly died. You tell me what kind of man does those things. You tell me how that says he loves you, and I'll back off and never say another word about it."

Erin stared at the front of the house, where the TV flickered through the open curtains in the living room window. She swallowed twice, an ache shoving into her throat. "He… he's not really there, right? I left the TV on?" Except she knew she hadn't. She'd never turned it on the night before, had closed and locked the door behind her when she left.

Her father was home and he hadn't bothered to check on her, even though he knew where she was, knew what had happened.

The world slowed, like time was slogging through creek mud. All of Jenna's words this week, all of Wyatt's over the years, all of Jason's just now… They all crashed in at once, clogging her thoughts and muddying the waters.

Her phone buzzed and she pulled it from the pocket of the jacket Wyatt had loaned her since her sweatshirt was covered in smoke and soot. That you out there? Time you got in here and watched out for someone besides yourself.

Erin let the phone fall against her leg and stared at the house. They were right. They were all right. She'd given her father everything she had, including her marriage to Jason, and none of it was enough. None of it had made him care.

None of it had made him love her.

Reaching across the console, Jason pulled Erin's phone from her numb fingers and read the screen before he slipped it into his jacket pocket. "We're done here." His voice was low and quiet. "Let's go." He shifted the truck into Reverse and backed out of the driveway as Erin stared straight ahead, not comprehending anything past the noise in her head.

He made a quick call to someone, but the words didn't compute past the buzz in her ears. They were almost back to town before he spoke to her. "You okay?"

"No." How could she be? Her entire life flashed by on fast-forward in her mind. Those days she'd been left standing on the curb at school, waiting until the teacher called Wyatt's parents. The way he belittled her job, her skills. The friends he'd driven away until she had none left.

Only Wyatt and Jenna had stuck by her.

And Jason…until she'd run him away. She sniffed and chewed on her bottom lip until it ached. For years she'd projected her father onto Jason, assuming he was selfish and needy and demanding. But he'd hung on, had stood by her until she'd crushed him. "I'm sorry."

"For what?"

There was too much. The words wouldn't come. She'd done so much to hurt him that no words seemed adequate. Erin simply shrugged and turned her face toward the window, numb to everything but the pain she'd caused Jason.

"Look, you need to get your head on straight and you need a shower and a change of clothes in a safe place." Jason wheeled the truck into a parking space in front of the small Mountain Springs Police Station. "I talked to Wyatt and he said to bring you here. This is about as safe as it gets for now. He's going to grab one of the on-duty officers and they'll go back to your house to get you some clothes so you can get a shower here and catch some rest where there's always somebody keeping watch. He said he'll talk to you later about what to do permanently."

What he didn't say caved in Erin's chest. Wyatt was taking another officer with him because her father wasn't going to like it when she didn't come home, and there was no telling what he'd do. "You think Dad is—"

"Your phone hasn't stopped buzzing since I put it in my pocket. I can promise you he's not happy." Jason shoved the door open and put one foot on the ground before he turned to look over his shoulder at Erin. He started to speak, but then he pulled his phone from his pocket and read the screen.

"Get inside. Now." He rounded the car and jerked her door open, then pulled her out by her bicep, urging her toward the building, his hand on his hip where his pistol likely rested.

Erin stumbled but kept her footing. "What's going on?" She couldn't keep the panic out of her voice. If he was acting this way, something was crazy wrong.

Jason opened the station door and practically shoved her inside. "Someone tried to kill Caroline Augustus."

Positioning himself between Erin and the road, Jason kept his hand on the Sig at his hip and urged her closer to the door. His ears strained for the sound of gunshots and his spine tensed against the smack of a bullet. Though the threat wasn't immediate, he could feel it deep inside. This was escalating, quickly. While the killer had never used direct tactics like gunfire before, anything was in the realm of possibility now.

He didn't get a deep breath until they were inside the station. Two police officers approached, one eyeing Erin with concern and the other eyeing him with suspicion.

The one closest to Erin addressed her. Officer Eaton, according to the name on his uniform. "Wyatt called and told us you guys were headed this way. Everything okay?"

Jason removed his hand from his pistol and held it out to the side. "In the immediate moment, yes. But we're going to have to camp out here with you guys for a bit until we figure out what's going on."

The other officer, Owens, stepped aside and pointed to a short hallway, as brightly lit as the front lobby area was. "There's a break room two doors up the hallway."

Jason thanked him, then turned toward Erin. She was rooted to the floor, staring at him as though she couldn't quite piece together everything that was happening.

He couldn't blame her. Things were moving too fast. The fire. Her father. Caroline. He needed to set the brakes and give them both a second to recover.

Erin opened her mouth, breathed in deeply, then exhaled. "Is Caroline okay?"

"For now. Someone tried to suffocate her, but the nurses came in when her alarms went off. No one was there." Reaching out to Erin, he laid a hand on the curve of her lower back and urged her toward the hallway, farther into the building and away from the glass front windows. They couldn't stand here in the open and dialogue. "Come on." He kept his voice low, hoping it would calm whatever was raging inside her. "We'll sit down. Grab some coffee. I can smell it from here."

She nodded once and let him guide her up the hall and into the room, where he pulled a metal folding chair away from a white plastic round table. Erin sat and stared at her hands. "Who texted you?"

Sliding into the chair next to hers, he reached for her hands and held them on the table, needing the connection to her. As out of control as her life was, his was spinning just as fast. He needed something to ground him and, as usual, Erin was the constant. She'd always been the constant. Even after their marriage fell to pieces and he was overseas fighting battles both physical and mental, she'd never been far from his mind.

Everything he'd done had been for her.

The thought drove his world to a grinding halt. He jerked his hands from hers and balled them in his lap. He'd joined the army for her. Worked his way up through the ranks to make more money to send to her. He'd never admitted it to himself, and he could never tell her.

Erin Taylor was the driving force of his life. And when the smoke cleared, he'd have to find a way to move forward, with or without her.

"Jason?" Her voice had steadied, seeming to come from a new place of strength. She ducked her head and caught his eye. "Who texted you?"

He'd forgotten she'd asked. Pulling his phone from his pocket to give him something to look at besides her, he pressed the screen. "Lisa. She's a nurse at the hospital and one of the nurses told her after she was released."

"I don't understand." The tortured look on Erin's face almost drove him around the table to pull her into his arms. He'd done this to her, had brought this mess down on her head. Now there was nothing he could do to stop it. "Why would someone do something so out in the open like that? There are video cameras everywhere."

"I think the attack on you proved that video cameras don't scare this guy."

She nodded once, then pulled a napkin from the holder in the center of the table and began shredding the edges. This was not the Erin he was used to. She was crumbling, her emotions finally exposed.

That was either a very good thing or a very, very bad thing.

He laid a hand on hers, trying to let her know without words that he was here for her, but she pulled away and went back to tearing the napkin. "Call her. See what she knows. Make sure she's okay. Because if somebody came after Caroline, then Lisa isn't safe either. And she doesn't have you watching her back the way I do."

True. Caroline had Caesar. Erin had Jason and Wyatt. Lisa had no one. He dialed her number and waited through the rings until the call went to voice mail, pressed End, then tried again.

Three tries and no answer.

Jason's jaw hurt from the tension. Caroline had been attacked. Lisa wasn't responding.

Something was very wrong.

This time, Erin reached for him, wrapping

her fingers around his and squeezing tight. "She's not answering?"

"No."

"Call Wyatt. Have him call—"

His phone vibrated in his hand and shot relief through him. "Maybe she was talking to someone at the hospital."

But when he glanced at the screen, the name that flashed across was from Caesar. At my apartment. Everything's sideways. Don't know what to do. Don't know how to fix this.

Pulling away from Erin, Jason rocketed to his feet, dialing Caesar's number as he did. The call went to voice mail, and as he scrolled through his contacts to find Caesar's landline number, another text popped up on the screen.

Help me.

Jason paced to the door and gripped the frame until his knuckles ached, his eyes fixed on Caesar's two-word plea. Caesar needed him.

He raised his head and stared at the ceiling in the hallway. Erin needed him.

As though she'd heard his thoughts, she was behind him, one hand on his back, the other reaching for his phone. She read the screen, shut her eyes for a moment, then handed it back to him. "Go."

"I can't take you with me." For all he knew, Caesar was behind all of this and the entire thing was a giant trap. But even with all of the evidence, Jason couldn't bring himself to believe one of his brothers was behind the murders.

"I'll be fine here. I seriously doubt anybody is going to storm the police station. And even if they did, I happen to know that Rand Webster is the best shot in three counties."

Jason reached for her and pulled her to his chest, resting his chin on the top of her head. The world was rarely divided into a strict right-or-wrong decision, but this one was too much. It was tearing him apart. Protect Erin? Or go to his buddy?

Erin planted her hands on his chest and eased away from him. "You have to go. I'll be fine. Really. Just let me know what's going on. And be careful."

The urge to kiss her nearly overwhelmed him, but if he did, he'd never let her go. Instead, he pressed his lips briefly to her forehead. Even that was almost enough to make him stay. "You're the bravest person I know."

"I learned it from you."

"Don't leave here. Not for anything." If something happened to her while he was gone…

He couldn't even consider that.

"I won't." She backed away from him, almost dismissing him. "Get going."

With one last look at her, Jason turned and sprinted up the hallway. Whatever was happening on the other end of his cell phone, he had no doubt the endgame was in sight and the bloodshed was likely going to get worse.

SIXTEEN

Jason paced the parking lot of Caesar's apartment complex. Two buildings away, police cars barricaded the way to Caesar's apartment. Someone had called 911 from Caesar's apartment and they'd been there when he arrived. The officers had barred him from going any farther. No amount of begging or showing them Caesar's texts had helped. He was blocked. Barred from helping Caesar. Nearly an hour away from Erin.

Helpless.

He'd hoped for a break after last night. Had prayed for a resolution, prayed the women would be safe and whoever was doing this would realize they'd been made and stop.

Far from it. Things were escalating, which meant Erin was in even more danger, and he was putting her at greater risk.

Now Caroline had nearly been killed. Lisa

wasn't answering her phone. Caesar's apartment was filled with police and paramedics.

And Jason was torn into pieces. He needed to be with Erin to watch over her. He needed to be here with Caesar.

Leaving Erin in the safety of the police station had nearly torn him in two. Right now, she was better off there than out here in the open with him. Better off with men who could actually protect her instead of constantly failing her. Instead of losing the guard on their mouths and spewing out the truth about her father in a way that left her shell-shocked.

Just like when Fitz was killed, Jason was in the center of the action, helpless, no matter what the outside world thought. The newspaper this morning had called Erin and him both heroes.

But only one of them was. The other was someone who'd wrecked everything he touched, who let people die when he could save them.

Tires rolled on the pavement behind him, as Wyatt arrived in a police cruiser, lights off, siren silent. He climbed out of the car and scanned the area. "Any news?"

"Not yet on my end. I can't get any closer than this."

"You made a good call leaving Erin at the station, although I know it was hard on you to make it. She'll be safe there. Eaton and Owens are good cops."

Something about Wyatt's demeanor was off. He couldn't look Jason in the eye but kept watching the area as though he searched for something. They'd been friends too long for him to have a successful poker face. He was withholding something.

"Tell me what you know." Jason had called Wyatt as he was leaving the station because he hadn't known where else to turn. There was one way to find out what was happening, and it was through Wyatt. He should apologize for using his friend, but Wyatt likely already knew.

"You first."

Fair enough. "Lisa Fitzgerald contacted me. She's a nurse at the hospital, and when she was released, she tried to visit Caroline and was denied access to the floor. One of the other nurses told her someone had tried to kill Caroline. I tried to call Lisa, got nothing, then got the texts from Caesar..." Jason swept his hand to encompass the entire scene before them. "Of course, nobody will tell me anything, but according to his text, Caesar is inside. It doesn't make sense. Why would he leave Caroline alone?"

"I can't answer that, but I do know a few things." Wyatt's voice was grim, and he walked back to the cruiser, where he leaned in and retrieved his phone. "I talked to a buddy on the sheriff's department, and I shouldn't say this, but…"

Adrenaline jolted Jason. If Wyatt was going to violate a confidence, this was worse than he'd thought. "You don't have to say anything. I shouldn't have called you."

"You need to know." Wyatt read his phone's screen for a bit before he looked back to the emergency responders. "Without giving you too many details, Tony Augustus left the hospital about an hour before his wife was attacked."

"Who was with her after he left?"

"No one."

Jason scanned the parking lot, the sky, the buildings in front of him, but none of it registered. Something wasn't right. "Who came after Caroline?"

"We don't know. The camera on her hallway was disabled."

"Why are the police here?"

"Someone in Caesar's apartment made a 911 call about half an hour ago, but they hung up. Officers have to check if they return a call and no one answers. The front door was cracked, so the responding officer entered."

Jason's gut twisted. Someone was in the apartment, and he had a horrible, sick feeling he knew who it was.

"Tony Augustus overdosed on opiates, Jase, probably right after he texted you. He's been taken to the hospital alive, but barely. He wrote a note that took responsibility for all of the murders."

Slamming a palm onto the roof of Wyatt's patrol car, Jason turned his back to the scene to stare across an open field beside the apartment complex, trying to keep his stomach from revolting. He had wanted an end to this, but not this way. Not with proof one of his buddies had taken innocent lives, destroyed families and shattered dreams.

Caesar had mentioned violent thoughts, but he'd never hinted at the desire to act on them or indicated they'd gotten so far out of control he couldn't reel them in.

If Caesar could crack like this, anybody could.

Even him.

His whole life had been a fight for control, particularly when he'd emancipated from his parents. Trying to get Erin to tell her father the truth, joining the army in order to prove he could provide for her... Everything he'd done for her was an act of control, of trying to protect her from a distance and to keep her from losing everything.

"Where's your head, Jase?"

The question echoed across the years, the same one Wyatt's father had asked many times when Jason had been battling his parents' abandonment. He almost smiled, because Wyatt's adult voice sounded exactly like his father's.

But these thoughts weren't worth smiling about.

Because no matter how much he loved Erin, he was still going to have to leave her in the end. He'd been right all along. The greatest danger to her was him.

"My head?" Jason addressed the brittle grass in the field. "I've seen the headlines. They're calling me a hero. Know what? They called all of us heroes when we came home, even Caesar. But I know the truth." He spun on his heel to face Wyatt. "The truth is, I'm a failure. I missed the signs and let my team get ambushed, let Fitz get killed. I had questions about Caesar from the moment Angie died and I kept them to myself. And who's to say I won't lose my head one day and turn out the same way? We went through the same experiences." He jabbed his finger at the flashing emergency lights. "Caesar is a good man, a crack soldier and a guy who always had my back. How did he get here? And what if I follow him?"

Wyatt crossed his arms and exhaled loudly, leaning back against the hood of the cruiser. "Far as I'm concerned, you're already out of your head."

The flat statement grabbed Jason's spinning thoughts and stopped them cold. "What?"

"I can't say what happened to your buddy. I have no idea what you went through overseas, but you're fine. Who knows why some people crack and some don't, but I'm betting if you go back and think hard, there were signs long before this." Wyatt shifted, planting his feet wider. "I'll tell you something my dad told me once, right after I got my badge. I saw a lot overseas, but the most afraid I ever felt was here, on a domestic call about a week in, when a guy fired shots at us out a window. Bullets were supposed to fly outside the wire downrange, but not here. It spooked me."

"How is this helping?" He didn't need a lecture. He needed to…to hit something. To find a gym and a punching bag and pour all of this pent-up anger and frustration on an inanimate object until he collapsed. Then maybe he could forget for a few minutes what he'd lost…and what he was about to lose when he walked away from Erin again.

"Heroes aren't fearless. Heroes aren't perfect. They see what needs to be done and they do it, even though they're scared. Even though they mess up. Brother, you've got to stop thinking you have to be perfect. The way you talk, you think you have to check the box before God will even listen to your prayers."

The words slammed into Jason, a fist to the stomach so lightning quick he nearly bent double. How did Wyatt know?

"You're blaming yourself for things other people have done of their own free will, things you're powerless to stop because you don't wear a cape and change clothes in a phone booth. Heroes get up when they're knocked down, Jase." Wyatt straightened and clapped a firm hand on Jason's shoulder. "Cowards run."

As though he'd given the definitive answer to life, Wyatt stepped around Jason and walked toward the crime scene, hailing a sheriff's deputy.

Jason watched him go, balling his fists, still desperate to hit something, desperate to understand everything happening.

Cowards run.

The words circled in his head, daring him to act.

Wyatt was right. He wasn't Caesar or Rich or Fitz or any other soldier. They'd all been together that day, had faced overwhelming odds, pinned down by evil men with evil intent. They'd all been wounded. The responsibility wasn't his alone.

Neither was the pain. They were all hurting, physically and emotionally. They'd all continue to hurt as news of Caesar's betrayal spread.

He could choose to live in the pain, or he could move forward with his life.

He could choose to stand even though he'd been knocked down.

He could keep relying on himself or, as he had in the fire, he could surrender his life to Jesus and trust Him for the next step, trusting the One who died because Jason could never be perfect.

This was a step he couldn't take alone.

He had to get to Erin, to tell her the truth about his feelings, about the money, about everything. On the way, he had a whole lot of praying to do. Firing off a quick text to Wyatt, Jason strode to his truck to head back to Mountain Springs and to his future.

* * *

She couldn't take it anymore.

Erin had paced the hallway of the police station until there had to be a ditch forming in the gray tile, her mind as mushy as the oatmeal it reminded her of. Everything about her life had changed in the past hour, her world rocked sideways by the truth.

Her father didn't love her. The father she'd loved her entire life, had sacrificed everything to protect.

That was what daughters did, right?

Oh, God, what's the right thing to do?

She'd been asking the question for an hour, racked with uncertainty. Submit to her father or protect herself? With her eyes opened by Jenna's assertions and Jason's truths, she could see clearly what had been a hazy thought in her art studio. She'd never been safe. Had never been allowed to be who God had called her to be. Had charted a faulty course based on lies, on duty instead of love.

She loved her father, whether he loved her or not. But their relationship was killing them both, and something had to change.

She had to talk to him. To confront him. To tell him to his face she was moving out—to where, she didn't know—but it was time for both of them to stand on their own two feet, for both of them to start living.

If not, the real Erin would be lost forever, along with the dreams God was renewing inside her. She was meant to do more than this, and even if her future didn't include Jason, it did include growing closer to her Savior... and following her calling as a full-time firefighter.

Footsteps at the far end of the hallway whirled her around. Officer Dan Weston strolled closer. "Wyatt's on the phone. You can take it in the chief's office. Said he tried to call your cell but Jason had it on him."

Her phone. Jason had taken it at the house. She whirled and headed up the hall, grabbing the phone and punching the button for the line on hold. "Wyatt?"

"It's over, Erin."

Erin sank into the seat behind the chief's desk and clinched the phone tighter. "Over?" She rocked backward, trying to let the news sink in. Her life was hers again. She didn't have to watch over her shoulder anymore. She was safe.

The realization was slow to take hold, and it brought more questions than answers. "What happened? Who was it?"

"I can't tell you right now. Jason's headed

back to my house. He wants you to meet him there. You can take my truck. Have Owens give you the keys."

If Jason was right about someone on his team being the killer and this was truly over, then the repercussions were bound to be slamming into Jason pretty hard. "How is he?"

"He needs you."

The words washed over her in a wave of relief and pain. Both of them had lost so much today, had lost so much in their lives. With so much changing, what was next for them? They needed each other. The truth was, she'd never stopped needing him. Had never truly stopped loving him. She'd merely shoved him aside out of guilt and a twisted sense of responsibility. And when everything had fallen apart, when she'd been in danger, her father hadn't been the one there for her.

Jason had. "He really did love me once."

"Once?" Wyatt chuckled, but it held no mirth. "Where do you think the grant money you've been getting all of these years came from?"

"What?"

"Whoa. No. I didn't say that."

Erin sank deeper into the chair, shock and grief robbing her muscles of their strength. "Jason was sending me money." It all made sense now. The amount had been small at first, growing at fairly regular intervals in a "cost-of-living increase." The money must have paced his salary as he rose through the ranks. The world started spinning, and she grabbed the edge of the desk, desperate to make it stop. "Why?"

Wyatt was silent, seeming to weigh how much he should say. "This isn't my story to tell. I shouldn't have—"

"Why?" If she went to Jason, he'd deny it. Wyatt was her source of information, and she had to know what she'd thrown away while listening to her father's lies.

The grief almost choked her.

Wyatt exhaled loudly. "Jason knew your paycheck as a firefighter wouldn't cover the bills, and he knew you'd probably let go of your dream if something didn't happen to stretch the money. Before he left, he had Dad help him arrange everything. I found out about it a few months ago, when I came across a bank statement Dad had left on the table and I put two and two together."

Jason had sacrificed for her, even after she'd booted him out of her life, had refused to be the wife he deserved. From living near Camp McGee, she had a vague idea of what a soldier made and the calculations told the tale. He'd been sending her a large chunk of his paycheck for years. Sacrificing his life so she could continue to live her dream.

Sacrificing himself in a way her father never had.

His actions made no sense, unless he'd stayed out of her way because he'd thought she wanted him gone. And why wouldn't he think she was over him? She'd told him so when she'd shut him out and sent him divorce papers, accusing him of abandoning her.

But he never had.

"Wyatt, I have to go." She hung up the phone and stared at the scarred desktop. She needed to see Jason, to tell him she knew and that she loved him. That she was sorry and she wanted to start over, if he'd have her.

But first she had to confront her father. There would be no rest until that happened. She'd go to Wyatt's and meet Jason…but only after she'd gone home first. Her father may have treated her badly, but he deserved to hear face-to-face why she was leaving.

She marched to the front desk and asked Officer Owens for Wyatt's keys. She wrapped her fingers tightly around them, her resolve deepening. "Thanks, Mike. If Wyatt calls back, tell him to let Jason know I'll be at the house in an hour. I've got something to take care of first."

"I don't think he'll like—"

Erin was already in motion, pushing past Owens on the way to the door. "He'll understand." When she hit sunlight, there was no pause to enjoy her freedom. Too much pain lay ahead.

Outside of town, she pushed the truck faster and prayed for wisdom, for the right words for her father, for forgiveness and God's will. This was tricky territory, pulling away from a parent.

But Jason had done it. The circumstances were different, to be sure, but necessary. She ached for him in a whole new way.

Slowing for the S-turn before the bridge over Redbill Creek, Erin glanced in the side-view mirror.

A dark sedan was close on her bumper. Where had he come from? Something about the car crawled over her skin, and she checked the rearview.

The windshield of the car was shattered, the hood bearing a deep dent in the center.

In the exact place Angie Daniels had landed when a dark sedan struck her.

White-hot fear raced through Erin's blood.

No. Wyatt said the threat was over. How could—

A tap on the rear bumper nosed the truck forward, and Erin gripped the steering wheel tighter, fighting for control. Few people traveled this road unless they were headed to the small community near her house, so the likelihood of help happening upon her was slim. She reached in her hip pocket for the phone, then drew back and grabbed the steering wheel again.

Jason still had it.

She was in this alone.

Either she had to outrun the car or slow down and pray the lack of speed would be enough to keep her from careening out of control if there was another hit.

The sedan tapped her again.

Erin's gaze leaped to the rearview mirror, trying to see the driver, but the cracked windshield made identification impossible.

As they drove into the S-turn, the car backed off. Erin breathed a sigh of relief, but as the bridge came into view, the sedan flew closer, engine revving into a roar as the car pulled even with Erin and slammed into the side of the truck.

The impact jolted her head sideways, her neck screaming in pain. Erin fought the wheel, trying to keep the truck in line. She was bigger, heavier, but the angle the car had her pinned was no match. She couldn't slam on the brakes or she risked a skid that would roll her into the side of the mountain looming above the road. The truck edged closer and closer to an unyielding wall of rock, the concrete bridge railing looming closer. If she hit the bridge head-on at this speed, no airbag in the world would save her.

Metal screeched as the other car kept pace with her, the force grinding her sideways.

Lifting her foot from the gas, Erin prayed for the best and jerked the wheel to the right at the last second, the embankment her only hope. If she could hit it at the right angle, the truck would run straight down to the creek, but she'd avoid the railing.

If she could keep…the front end…straight…

The car slammed on the brakes, taking away the pressure she'd been fighting. The steering wheel jerked sideways, and the side of the truck clipped the bridge railing, throwing her off center and sending the truck rolling down the embankment.

Front and side airbags deployed, throwing Erin in multiple directions as the world turned over and over. She choked on vertigo and dust and panic, the spin lasting a lifetime before the truck came to rest.

Erin shoved the limp airbag from her face and gasped for air, fear rising until she got a deep breath.

She'd landed right side up in Redbill Creek. She was safe.

Until whoever had run her off the road found a way to finish the job. She knew how this worked. They wouldn't leave her alive.

Fighting nausea from the roll down the hill, her face throbbing and her entire body aching, Erin managed to unbuckle the seat belt, but when she moved her left arm to open the door, pain ripped through her. She bit back a scream as dark spots crossed her vision. Her wrist throbbed, increasing the pain jolting through her.

But she couldn't stop now. She had to get out, to hide in the woods, to get to the road for help.

She reached across with her right hand, opened the door and stumbled into the creek. Water rushed to her knees, the cold mountain current sending an instant ache into her legs.

"That's far enough."

Erin whirled toward the creek bank at the sound of a woman's voice, but the motion wobbled and dropped her to her knees in the water, the cold rising to her chest and ripping her breath away.

Lisa Fitzgerald stood about ten feet away, a revolver leveled at Erin's head.

With nothing to grab on to, the current of the creek tugged against Erin. She wobbled. "Lisa?" This was a hallucination. It had to be. Lisa was a victim. Her house had burned. Caroline was her friend. Why would—

Lisa slogged closer and shoved the pistol into the back of her pants.

Maybe she was here to help.

Erin lifted her good hand as Lisa edged closer, but the other woman regarded it with disdain. "It's sad, Erin. To survive a violent wreck only to drown."

Before Erin could move, Lisa circled behind her, grabbed her hair and shoved her beneath the water.

SEVENTEEN

"Dispatch called. My truck sent out an accident call from the bridge over Redbill Creek. How close are you?"

Jason's fingers tightened around his cell phone as Wyatt spoke, his tight voice betraying his emotions. The only person who would be in Wyatt's truck was Erin.

If she was near the creek, she'd been headed home, not to Wyatt's house the way he'd asked. Slowing his truck, Jason hooked a J-turn in the road and raced back toward the creek, pushing his pickup to the red zone. "Maybe three minutes."

"I've got guys en route, but you're closer. They're maybe five minutes behind you. I'm on my way. This isn't right."

No, it wasn't. Jason killed the call and threw the phone onto the passenger seat, gripping the steering wheel with both hands. What was Erin thinking heading back to her father's house alone? The man wasn't dangerous, but Jason wouldn't put it past him if pushed. He'd heard enough stories in the past about bar fights and altercations around town to know Kevin Taylor wasn't beyond throwing a punch.

He was at the bridge over Redbill Creek in two minutes, slowing as he approached.

There was no sign of Wyatt's truck.

Maybe dispatch was wrong? He was reaching for the phone to call Wyatt when he rolled onto the bridge. Blue paint marred the concrete railing. Trees and vines were broken off and shredded.

She'd gone over the side.

He was out of the truck while it was still rocking from the quick stop. He peered over the bridge, his pulse thundering. Wyatt's truck, smashed and dented almost beyond recognition, sat in the creek, the driver's door hanging open, the cab empty. So where—

There. A person stood in the creek, bent at the waist.

But it wasn't Erin. The woman, with blond hair straggling out of a black baseball cap, was leaning over something in the river.

Something that was thrashing. Struggling.

Adrenaline slammed through his veins. This wasn't over. Caesar wasn't the killer.

The killer had Erin.

He half slid, half ran down the embankment, branches slapping at his face and digging into his skin, making enough noise to draw the attention of everyone in a three-mile radius.

As soon as his feet hit the flat bank, the woman turned toward him, a gun aimed straight at his chest.

Lisa.

What?

The moment froze, reality jumbling. Why was Lisa here? What was she doing?

"Jason?" Her eyes widened, and her voice rose with panic. She released her hold on Erin and stepped closer to Jason, the gun lowering. Multiple emotions ranged across her face.

Erin rose from the water at chest level, gasping and coughing, her eyes wild and panicked.

Turning away from Lisa, Jason dived for Erin, splashing into the water, the current slowing him as he slogged toward her. She had to be okay. He couldn't lose her now.

But Lisa…?

Lisa backed away, her gaze bouncing between Erin and Jason, her expression tight. "What are you— I was—" Something crossed her face, a determination that bordered on hardness. Calculated hardness. "I was driving by. Saw a truck go over the bridge. It was flying. I came to—" She raised the weapon again, leveling it on Jason's chest. "Stop."

He was a few feet from Erin but he staggered to a halt, fighting to keep his balance in creek water over his knees. Lisa was unhinged. She was as likely to shoot Erin as she was to shoot him, and he couldn't risk either of their lives.

Behind Lisa, Erin gasped for air, then stabilized, her eyes finding Jason's. Her left hand stayed low in the water, but she held up her right in a motion that indicated he should obey Lisa. "I'm okay."

"This is not good." Lisa muttered the words to herself, eyes shifting between Erin and Jason.

Jason slowly raised his hands. Give her what she wanted. Let her think she had control. He needed time to think. Time to get the last seven or eight feet without her firing.

The water would slow him, and as long as she held a weapon, she had the advantage. "What's not good?" Maybe he could get her talking, distract her.

"You. Here. You weren't supposed to see this, to watch me take out the last thing standing between us. You weren't supposed to know I brought us together."

Whoa. "What?"

Erin wavered, and Jason lunged for her, but Lisa turned the gun away from Jason to Erin.

"Let me think!" The gleam in her eye turned hot with anger, and the gun shook as it wavered inches from Erin's face. Lisa swallowed, her attention on Jason. "You. All of you on Jonathan's team took away what was precious to me. You let my husband die. You killed him."

"Lisa, you have no idea what you're—"

"Now I've taken away what was precious to all of you."

The words slammed into Jason's chest. Lisa blamed them for Fitz's death? Had killed Angie and the others? With a roaring clarity, Fitz's words as they'd geared up for their last mission came back. *Lisa's not handling these deployments well. When we get back, I'm looking at units that will let me be with her, get her the help she needs.*

Fitz hadn't come back to make good on his promise. And for the first time since the day Fitz died, Jason didn't bear the guilt. "We didn't kill him. We were—"

"But you didn't save him. I wanted you all to hurt like I hurt. To face life with your future destroyed. But you…" She swung the gun toward Jason again. "You were there for me. You knew I needed you. You're the reason I moved here. But there *she* was… In the way. Keeping me from being happy again. This is her fault. And yours. I'd have killed her the night I hit Angie if you hadn't been in the way."

Erin gasped. "That's why you stopped. You didn't want to kill Jason."

"No. I needed him."

"Lisa, let me help you again. We'll find someone you can talk to about this." Jason edged closer, praying she'd view the gesture as a friendly one. If he could get two more feet, he'd be in reach and…

She shifted the gun again, the barrel in Erin's face, her eyes on Jason. "Fitz said the same thing the last time he came back. Told me I should talk to somebody. Should take my meds. I've been hearing it for years. From him, from my parents, from everybody."

Erin tilted her head, catching his attention. She flicked her glance to Lisa and back again.

She was going to go for it, try to take Lisa out.

Before he could shake his head no, sirens crossed the distance from the direction of town. Help was coming.

But not fast enough.

As Lisa's head turned toward the sound, Erin launched herself sideways, her shoulder slamming into Lisa's stomach, but the awkward tug of the water robbed her of momentum. The gun fired as Lisa staggered and stumbled backward into the water.

Erin cried out.

As the sirens grew louder, Jason lunged, trying to get between Erin and Lisa, calculating how to take out a woman he'd once considered a friend.

Shouts rang across the creek bed and police officers stormed the area, dragging Lisa upright as Jason reached Erin.

He gathered her close, pulling her to him, burying his face in her damp hair. "Are you hit?"

"I'm fine. Just my wrist." She wrapped one arm around his waist, her head nestled into the hollow of his neck, her body warm and trembling against his.

The chaos around them faded away. Erin was safe.

"I don't need emergency transport." Erin pulled the blanket tighter around her and held it at her neck with her right hand, shrugging off Chief Kelliher as he and one of the para-

medics tried to usher her toward the open
door of a waiting ambulance. "I can ride in
one of the trucks." She didn't want to leave
as a priority case, sirens blaring. It was em-
barrassing to be the one being fussed over.

But even more, there was no way she was
leaving on anyone's terms but her own. Not
without seeing Jason, not without telling him
he couldn't leave her again.

Officers had separated them in the water
and helped her onto the bank. She'd lost sight
of him as the first responders checked her
wrist and splinted it. He could leave before
she got to him.

She couldn't let that happen.

Because she knew if she left the creek
without talking to him, without telling him
she chose him, then she'd lose him. She had
to apologize. Tell him she'd been wrong.

So many words to say. Words that sounded
like *I love you. Let's try this again.* The idea
of being married to Jason again, of being by
his side legitimately, as the one he loved for
the rest of their lives, seemed natural and
right. It wasn't enough to be close to him.
She wanted to belong to him again.

"I need Jason."

The chief laid a hand on her arm and turned
her to face him. "You need to get checked out

for a concussion. And get to the hospital to have your lungs—"

"Jason first."

"I'm here." His deep, confident voice washed over her with an electric jolt.

He hadn't left. He'd come back for her.

Hope took flight.

As Chief Kelliher stepped to the side, Jason took his place, his blue eyes dark with concern. "You okay?"

"Sprained wrist." The words barely made their way out past the emotion in her throat. Here he was, standing right in front of her, the living embodiment of a thousand dreams she had squashed under her father's fist.

The dreams that flared back to life the longer he stood near her, his warmth palpable across the scarce inches between them.

It was a warmth she had to touch. Reaching out, she laid her palm on his chest, his shirt damp from their struggle in the water, his heart accelerating beneath her touch.

He swallowed twice, his Adam's apple bobbing, but he didn't speak, simply studied her with an expression that echoed her own emotions.

It was as though they'd both found hope but were hesitant to fully embrace it.

Erin wasn't letting fear hold her back. It had cost her too much in the past.

But Jason moved before she could. He wrapped his fingers around hers, pulling her hand tighter against his chest. "The other night, before the fire, when we were talking, I never finished what I started to say."

"Neither did I."

He scanned her face from her hair to her chin, before he met her eyes again. He eased closer, until the space between them was gone. His head tipped to one side and he let his gaze slide to her lips again, asking permission.

Erin rose on tiptoe, her nose brushing his, her lips a whisper from his. "Anytime you want. I don't care who's watching."

His breath hitched, and he brushed his lips against her ear. "I love you, Erin Taylor."

She didn't answer, just slid her cheek along his until their lips met, wrapping her good arm around his neck to pull him closer as his arms encircled her, protecting her, promising her more than either of them could put into words, but what both of them knew.

Their story began now.

EIGHTEEN

"Sometimes I think, despite your beautifully defined exterior, a little old man lives inside of you."

"What?" Jason's laugh warmed the air in the truck, leaving her to marvel at how far they'd come, and how he was hers once again.

"We're like an old couple out for a Sunday drive." Erin reached across the console of Jason's pickup and laced her fingers with his. Her left wrist, recently freed from the half cast that had stabilized it for the past month, held a dull ache from the sprain, but she hardly noticed it. She was still getting used to this new reality where she could once again reach out and touch the man she loved, where holding hands and even kisses were no longer taboo.

This time, they didn't have to be stolen. This afternoon, after church at Hill Street Chapel, he'd stood chatting with Chief Kelliher, his arm wrapped firmly around her shoulders for the world to see. Then they'd gone to visit Wyatt's parents, where she'd been living for the past month, for family dinner and afternoon football.

She'd loved every second of it.

She'd loved every second they'd spent together since they'd nearly lost one another in Redbill Creek. Since he'd returned to duty at Camp McGee, he'd spent every free moment in Mountain Springs with her. It was the relationship they should have had if her father hadn't intervened.

Erin's eyebrows drew together. In the beginning, her father had called and texted and threatened, always demanding, never listening to what she had to say. She'd ended each conversation with a firm *I love you, Dad* before hanging up on his latest tirade.

Two weeks ago, after she'd told him in a phone conversation she'd once been married to Jason, he'd stopped communicating at all, on the same day Wyatt brought word Lisa Fitzgerald had confessed to everything.

She'd been the one to plant evidence on Angie Daniels's phone and to drug Seth the night of the murder, to threaten Seth's life if Angie didn't obey her orders. Had drugged Tracy Dawson and left her car running in the garage… Had befriended then drugged Crystal Palmer and Amber Ransom as well.

Caesar had left the hospital after Lisa threatened Caroline's life and had written his confession as she stood over him with a gun, detailing her plans to kill his wife if he didn't do as she said. Both had recovered and were working through their traumas at home and overseas with a counselor and a chaplain.

"Hey. No sad faces allowed. We're Sunday driving, remember? It's supposed to be peaceful or something, right?" Jason squeezed her fingers, then let go to navigate a turn onto a narrow dirt road that wound through the woods.

Erin watched the trees pass, the surroundings growing more familiar. It had been years since she'd allowed herself to visit this place, but there was no doubt where they were. This was Campground Road. Through a break in the trees would stand an old tin-roofed farmhouse, likely in worse shape than she remembered. The one she'd stopped painting. The one that had once been the center of so many dreams.

Her face heated. "What are you doing?" If he was bringing her out here, well… She couldn't imagine where his head was. Didn't want to be disappointed by assuming she knew.

He shot her a quick grin, then let the truck glide to a stop at the edge of a clearing.

The one-story farmhouse dominated the edge of a broad field. The wood siding was covered with pristine white vinyl. The tin roof shone a cheery red. The overgrown yard had been mowed and edged.

Light shone from every pristine, unbroken window.

Erin couldn't tear her eyes from the sight. Her fingers dug into her knees as Jason shifted the truck into Park and shut off the engine. "Who did this?"

Without a word, Jason got out of the truck, came around to her side and opened the door. Grabbing her hand, he reached across her to unbuckle the seat belt, then pulled her to follow him. "I'd say I did it, but the truth is slightly different." Drawing her onto the porch, he stopped at the door and turned to her, one hand on the door and the other wrapped around hers. "A lot of people in this community love you. You've fought hard, have saved homes and lives, have cheered on your fellow firefighters, and when I bought this place, a lot of them chipped in to—"

"You bought this place?" Her heart staccatoed in her chest.

He'd bought the place of her dreams. He'd brought her here. That could only mean...

Stepping away from her, he swung the door open and ushered her inside with a hand on her lower back.

Erin stepped onto gleaming hardwood floors into a huge open living room and kitchen, void of furniture or appliances but freshly painted and spotless.

Empty...except for her easel and paints clustered in the center of the space. On the easel rested her unfinished painting of this very house.

She'd been aching to paint again since Jason had unlocked her heart. But she'd assumed she'd have to start over, to repurchase everything, that her father—who hadn't even let her come back for her clothes—had shut her away from them forever.

Tears threatened to choke her as she turned toward Jason, who stood directly behind her. "How?"

"Wyatt and his dad and your uncle Joe and I have been talking to your father. It's taken a lot of discussions. A lot. And some police presence, but... He's coming around. Slowly. He called me yesterday and told me to come and get these. While I was there, I told him I'd bought this place and I wanted you to live here." Reaching for her hand, he tugged her closer and rested his forehead against hers. "With me. As the wife I can parade in front of everybody in town. Marry me? Again?"

Cupping his face in her hands, Erin stood on tiptoe and pressed her lips to his, her silent *yes* putting an end to the restless wandering of her heart.

* * * * *

*If you enjoyed this story,
look for other books
by Jodie Bailey:*

Christmas Double Cross
Calculated Vendetta
Dead Run

Dear Reader,

For the past year, God has laid Psalm 139 on my heart, particularly the end of verse 13, "thou hast covered me in my mother's womb."

Some of us had two amazing, loving earthly parents. Some had one. Some had none. Here is the thing God has shown me, and I wanted to make sure it came through in Erin's and Jason's lives… No matter the kind of earthly parents you have, God is always, always there. We simply have to look for Him. Yes, in the midst of our trials and struggles and hurts, He can be hard to see. But when we look back, I'm certain hindsight shows us His fingerprints all over our lives. His little gifts are everywhere, and He sends people into our lives to fill in the missing pieces, even though we may not get to see exactly what those people did until we get to heaven.

If you are feeling unloved, unwanted, uninvited, know this… God Almighty loves you so big. And He cares about you so much that when you were hidden from sight, growing into life, He was watching you. Verse 16 goes on to say that He knew every single day of your life before you were even born into it.

I don't know about you, but that speaks of a deep love to me, a love that has been there every time we've laughed and every time we've cried. Every time life has been perfect and every time we've wondered why on earth God is letting this happen to us. It may not feel like He is always there, but, sweet one, from one who has seen some dark times herself, I promise you that He always is. We simply have to look.

I wish I could sit across from you, share a cup of coffee (or tea, if that's your thing) and tell you why I know this to be true. But I'm praying for you, that God sends you someone to help you if you're hurting. If you're healed, I'm praying you are the one that God sends. Let's be His love to one another and help each other see His light in the darkness.

I'd love to hear your God story, if you'd like to share it. Stop by www.jodiebailey.com and visit. You can find my story there, too, if you want to make yourself some coffee (or tea!) and check it out.

Jodie Bailey

Get 4 FREE REWARDS!

We'll send you 2 FREE Books
<u>plus</u> 2 FREE Mystery Gifts.

Love Inspired® books feature contemporary inspirational romances with Christian characters facing the challenges of life and love.

FREE Value Over **$20**

Counting on the Cowboy
Shannon Taylor Vannatter

Reunited by a Secret Child
Leigh Bale

YES! Please send me 2 FREE Love Inspired® Romance novels and my 2 FREE mystery gifts (gifts are worth about $10 retail). After receiving them, if I don't wish to receive any more books, I can return the shipping statement marked "cancel." If I don't cancel, I will receive 6 brand-new novels every month and be billed just $5.24 for the regular-print edition or $5.74 each for the larger-print edition in the U.S., or $5.74 each for the regular-print edition or $6.24 each for the larger-print edition in Canada. That's a savings of at least 13% off the cover price. It's quite a bargain! Shipping and handling is just 50¢ per book in the U.S. and 75¢ per book in Canada*. I understand that accepting the 2 free books and gifts places me under no obligation to buy anything. I can always return a shipment and cancel at any time. The free books and gifts are mine to keep no matter what I decide.

Choose one: ☐ **Love Inspired® Romance Regular-Print** (105/305 IDN GMY4) ☐ **Love Inspired® Romance Larger-Print** (122/322 IDN GMY4)

Name (please print)

Address   Apt. #

City   State/Province   Zip/Postal Code

Mail to the Reader Service:
IN U.S.A.: P.O. Box 1341, Buffalo, NY 14240-8531
IN CANADA: P.O. Box 603, Fort Erie, Ontario L2A 5X3

Want to try two free books from another series! Call 1-800-873-8635 or visit www.ReaderService.com.

*Terms and prices subject to change without notice. Prices do not include applicable taxes. Sales tax applicable in N.Y. Canadian residents will be charged applicable taxes. Offer not valid in Quebec. This offer is limited to one order per household. Books received may not be as shown. Not valid for current subscribers to Love Inspired Romance books. All orders subject to approval. Credit or debit balances in a customer's account(s) may be offset by any other outstanding balance owed by or to the customer. Please allow 4 to 6 weeks for delivery. Offer available while quantities last.

Your Privacy—The Reader Service is committed to protecting your privacy. Our Privacy Policy is available online at www.ReaderService.com or upon request from the Reader Service. We make a portion of our mailing list available to reputable third parties that offer products we believe may interest you. If you prefer that we not exchange your name with third parties, or if you wish to clarify or modify your communication preferences, please visit us at www.ReaderService.com/consumerschoice or write to us at Reader Service Preference Service, P.O. Box 9062, Buffalo, NY 14240-9062. Include your complete name and address.

LI18